THE AUTHOR Richard Tames studied history at Cambridge and took his Master's degree at the University of London, where he worked for over 15 years and was three times a Teacher Fellow. He now lectures for the London programs of Syracuse University and the American University and is a London Tourist Board registered "Blue Badge" guide. He is the author of *A Traveller's History of London*, *Bloomsbury Past*, *Soho Past*, and *The City of London Past.*

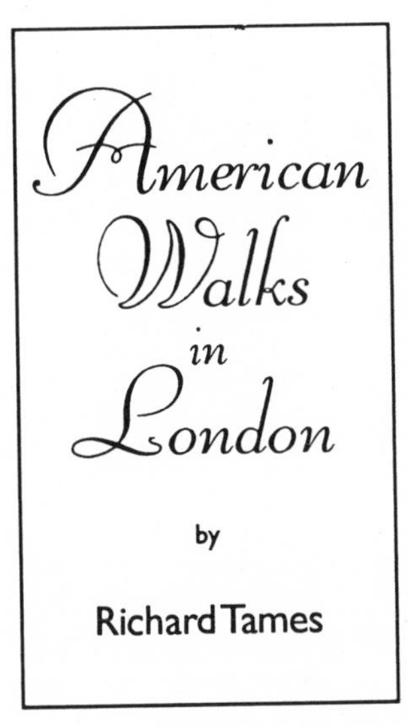

Ten
Step-by-Step
Itineraries for
North American
Visitors

INTERLINK BOOKS
An imprint of Interlink Publishing Group, Inc.
NEW YORK

First American edition published 1997 by
INTERLINK BOOKS
An imprint of Interlink Publishing Group, Inc.
99 Seventh Avenue
Brooklyn, New York 11215

Published simultaneously in Great Britain by The Windrush Press

Library of Congress Cataloging-in-Publication Data
Tames, Richard.
American walks in London : ten step-by-step itineraries for North American visitors / Richard Tames.
p. cm.
Includes bibliographical references and index.
ISBN 1-56656-213-9
1. Americans–Travel–England–London–Guidebooks.
2. Walking–England–London–Guidebooks. 3. London (England)–Tours.
I. Title.
DA679.T36 1997
914.2104'859–dc20 96-20498
CIP

Printed and bound in the United States of America

10 9 8 7 6 5 4 3 2 1

Contents

Introduction: Looking for London

> *"If many of the subjects discussed in these pages are without the charm of novelty, it is hoped the light in which they are viewed will give them, to some minds, more distinct and genial tints."*
>
> Henry T. Tuckerman, *A Month in England* (1853).

When New York writer Helen Hanff came to London for the publication of her book *84 Charing Cross Road,* she spent so much of her month in the capital looking out places she had read about that, on the eve of her departure, she realized the list had been so long that she *still* hadn't been to the Tower of London. As American novelist Paul Theroux, himself a long-time Londoner, has observed, London must be the most written-about city in the world. Because it has been written about, it has been read about and visitors come in search of a city they already feel they know. They may regret the absence of the murky fogs they associate with Sherlock Holmes (the invention of a Scot) or Jekyll and Hyde (invented by another Scot), or the pearly-buttoned, cheery cockneys depicted by the creators of Eliza Doolittle (an Irishman) or Mary Poppins (an Australian). But London should not disappoint. It is full of surprises. And you can never know it all.

London has been a magnet for talent and a crucible of enterprise throughout its two thousand-year history. Shakespeare never wrote a line before he came to London or after he left it. In the older parts of the capital almost every street has borne the imprint of a famous name, many drawn to the metropolis from far away. Chelsea alone has been home to Sir Thomas More, Tobias Smollett, Leigh Hunt, Oscar Wilde, Thomas Carlyle, Sir Alexander Fleming, "Scott of the Antarctic," J. M. W. Turner, George Eliot, Dante Gabriel Rossetti, Dylan Thomas, Mick Jagger, the creators of Dracula, and James Bond - not to mention, among Americans, Henry James, Mark Twain, T. S. Eliot, and painters John Singer Sargent and J. A. M. Whistler, and sculptor Jacob Epstein.

The ten walks in this book take in the main sights and a hundred by-ways as well. All of them begin and end at an Underground (Tube) station. You may find it very advisable to read the walk right through before you start, rather than as you go along. Or, at least, read the end sections with their suggestions for "delays and diversions," refreshments and shopping.

I can do all of these walks in under two hours, a number in less than an hour. But take your time. Allowing for refreshment and reflection, most might reasonably take a morning or an afternoon.

Become your own expert guide. Read on. Walk on. Enjoy.

Richard Tames
London

Note: (£) denotes admission charge

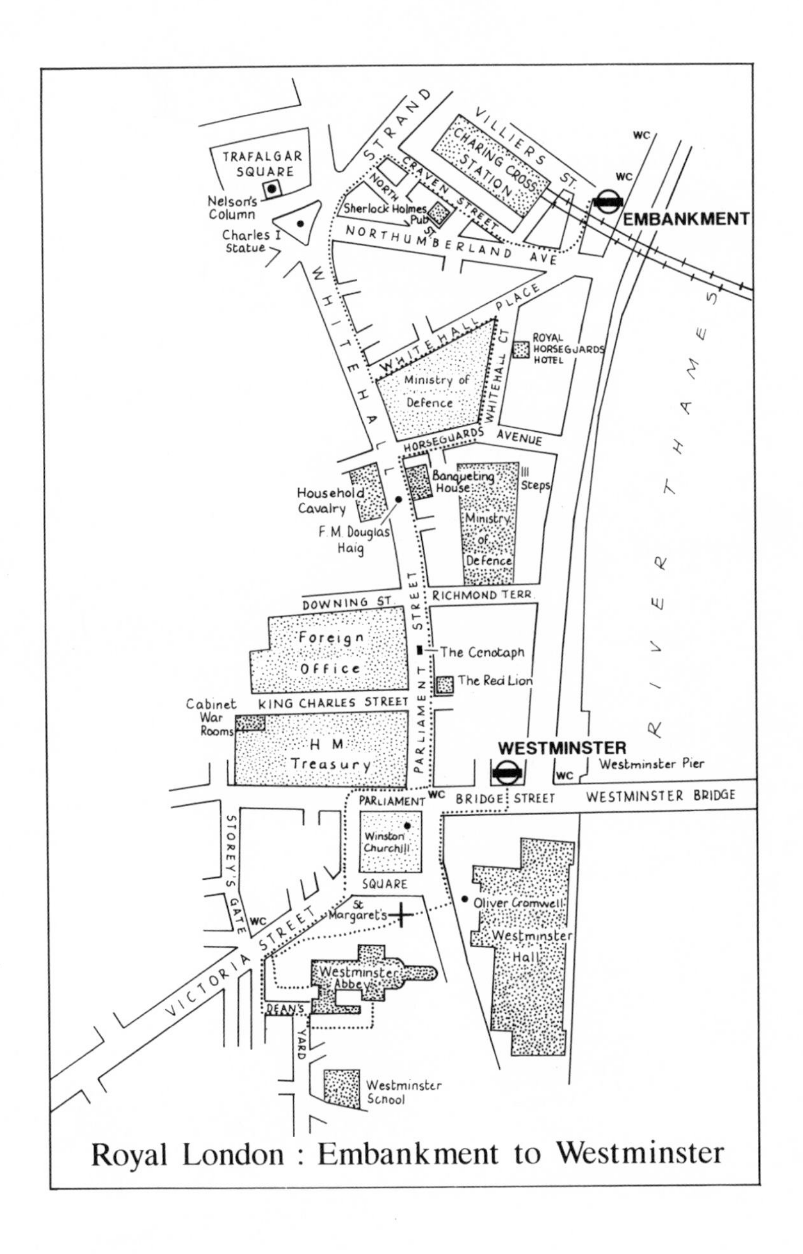

Royal London : Embankment to Westminster

1

Royal London: Embankment to Westminster

This walk passes through the heart of political London, taking in such famous sights as Trafalgar Square, Nelson's Column, the National Gallery, the Horse Guards, 10 Downing St., the Houses of Parliament, and Westminster Abbey. This part of London is almost always crowded and noisy, except early in the morning, but you are never far from Embankment Gardens or St. James's Park, well-tended oases of calm.

Starting Point - the ticket-hall of Embankment station (Circle or District lines)
After passing through the ticket-barriers turn left into Villiers St. and pause outside No. 43, named in honor of writer **Rudyard Kipling** (1865–1936), the first English language writer to win the Nobel Prize for Literature (1907). Arriving from India at 24, Kipling conquered literary London from a three-room apartment here. His reputation was confirmed by *Barrack Room Ballads* in 1892 and that same year he married Caroline Balestier, sister of American publisher Wolcott Balestier. The newly-weds moved to Vermont but failed to "settle" - an uncomfortable experience which convinced Kipling that Americans really were "foreigners". Kipling's literary standing nose-dived in the inter-war period, but subsequent generations have delighted in film versions of his children's classic *The Jungle Book* and adventurous tales of Indian life, such as *Kim* and *The Man Who Would Be King*.

The statue of Boadicea about ten years after it was unveiled in 1909. The souvenir seller charged for use of his telescope to view Big Ben in close-up.

Return towards the station, turn right under the railway bridge and then right again into Craven St. In 1849, **Herman Melville** (1819–91) lodged at No. 25, hoping to find a London publisher for his novel *White Jacket*, based on his service aboard the man o'war *United States*. Arriving in November, he was met by weather which fulfilled every American's worst (best?) expectations – "the old-fashioned pea soup London fog – of a gamboge colour." Weeks of bargaining followed, with Melville idling away the days between meetings by endlessly exploring London's lanes and back-alleys. He was eventually delighted to receive an advance of $900. In 1808, the adventurer and former Vice-President **Aaron Burr**

(1756–1836) lodged briefly at No. 30 before moving to the home of radical philosopher **Jeremy Bentham.** Burr, traveling as "G. H. Edwards," hoped to seduce the British government into supporting a lunatic scheme to conquer Cuba and Florida from the Spanish. The British, forewarned, at first kept him talking, then turned down his application for citizenship without explanation, then imprisoned him and finally expelled him as "embarrassing to His Majesty's government."

When **Benjamin Franklin** (1706–90) lived here at No. 36 (1757–62 and 1765–75), the waters of the Thames lapped at the very bottom of the street. Franklin acted as London representative not only of his native Pennsylvania, but also of Massachusetts, New Jersey, and Georgia, living in some style and moving in cultured company. His scientific interests made him a respected member of the Royal Society, while his political role brought him the friendship of British supporters of American liberty, such as Edmund Burke, Charles James Fox, and **William Pitt the Elder,** Earl of Chatham (1708–78). (Pittsburgh, Pa. grew up around Fort Pitt, named in honor of this Pitt, architect of the astounding victories which brought Canada and India under British rule in the Anglo-French global struggle of 1756–63.) Chatham called on Franklin here in person in a last-ditch attempt to avert colonial rebellion by suggesting that the Continental Congress be recognized as an official and permanent institution to represent American interests. Franklin confessed that "such a visit from so great a man, on so important a business, flattered not a little my vanity." Parliament, however, would have none of Chatham's proposal and Burke's moving speech on the need for reconciliation proved similarly abortive. Franklin's last day in Craven St. was spent in the company of **Joseph Priestley** (1733–1804), discoverer of oxygen. Priestley's unorthodox religious and political views later so roused the fury of an English mob that he fled to exile in America. As

Franklin left, literally weeping at the prospect of a civil war within the British Empire, he predicted that the struggle would last ten years - and America would win.

At the top of Craven St. turn left along the Strand, cross Northumberland Avenue, turn left into Whitehall and pause to note the equestrian statue of **Charles I**. A plate set behind its base marks the official geographical center of London, from which all distances are measured. Whitehall, lined with government ministries, is now synonymous with government itself. Three hundred years ago Whitehall Palace, an immense jumble of buildings with some 2,000 rooms, sprawled along either side of what is now London's widest thoroughfare. In 1698, a careless laundry-maid, drying clothes too close to a fire, started a blaze which burned down almost everything except the magnificent neo-Classical Banqueting House (see p. 5). The building now occupied by a pizzeria was, in the first decade of the twentieth century, an emigration office tempting Britons to occupy the empty lands of the Canadian prairie. The exodus reached its peak between 1911 and 1913, when over 400,000 left Britain annually - an outflow equal to one percent of the entire population leaving each year.

Continue down Whitehall, turn left down Whitehall Place and right into Whitehall Court. What is now the Royal Horseguards Hotel once housed the Authors' Club, where Pulitzer Prize-winner **Thornton Wilder** (1897-1975) took a room in 1948 but found devastated post-war London so deeply depressing that he hastened on to Paris. Playwright **George Bernard Shaw** (1856-1950) kept a London base here for some twenty years.

At the western end of Whitehall Court cross the road to see the steps which once led down from Whitehall Palace to the Thames. Until the 1860s the river came up this far; all the land between the stairs and the river was reclaimed when the Embankment was built in the 1860s to incorporate London's new sewer system and underground railway. The statues you can see from here are: standing pensively, imperial soldier-mystic **General Charles Gordon** (brilliantly portrayed by Charlton Heston in the film *Khartoum*); scanning the skies, **Lord Portal**, commander of the Royal Air Force in World War Two; and, standing at attention, **Lord Trenchard**, creator of the RAF in World War One. Beyond Trenchard an obelisk topped by a Chinthe, the mythical guardian of Burmese temples, commemorates the Chindits, a cosmopolitan force (including U.S. units), which fought behind Japanese lines in Burma in World War Two, commanded by the charismatic but erratic **Orde Wingate**, whose additional contribution to Israeli independence is also noted on the monument's inscription.

Turn right up Horse Guards Avenue and left back into Whitehall to pause in front of the Banqueting House (£), completed by London-born Welshman **Inigo Jones** in 1622. Under James I (reigned 1603–25) extravagant masques were staged here, with sets, costumes, and effects by Jones and scripts and choreography by Ben Jonson (1573–1637). The costs were horrendous – up to £2,000 each, enough to build a warship. In 1635, the Flemish artist **Peter Paul Rubens** (1577–1640) painted a series of stunning ceiling panels, extolling the virtue, wisdom, power, and glory of the ruling Stuart dynasty. Charles I, one of Europe's leading art connoisseurs, rewarded him with £3,000 and a knighthood. Charles's collection of paintings, depicting pagan, Catholic, or nude subjects, outraged Puritans as much as his father's masques had. With a fine sense of irony Oliver Cromwell (1599–1658) had the king executed here on January 30, 1649. The diminutive (4 ft. 11 ins.) monarch donned two shirts, lest he shiver from cold and appear afraid of the axe, and met his end with calm dignity.

On the opposite side of the road the Household Cavalry mounts guard daily in uniforms dating from the reign of George IV (reigned 1820–1830), the Life Guards in red,

The funeral of the Unknown Warrior 1920. King George V unveils the Cenotaph. The coffin containing the body of the Unknown Warrior, covered by the Union Jack, lies on a gun carriage to the right.

the Blues and Royals in blue. In the middle of the road stands an equestrian statue of **Field-Marshal Douglas Haig** (1861–1928), commander of the British Army during World War One; curiously, the horse is depicted in a stylized manner and the man naturalistically, but incorrectly, hatless. Haig, a taciturn Scot, prided himself on speaking French but it was alleged that this merely made him inarticulate in two languages. His unswerving faith in victory sustained him through a policy of attrition which condemned over 40 percent of all his troops to becoming casualties. He atoned after the war by founding Britain's veterans' organization, the Royal British Legion, and establishing the Haig Fund for the relief of the war-wounded. The artificial poppies made by disabled ex-servicemen and sold each autumn to raise cash for their benefit still bear his name.

Continue along Whitehall and note the statues outside the gray Ministry of Defence building. **"Uncle Bill" Slim** (1891–1970), clad in jungle fatigues, was a soldiers' general and the only Allied commander to beat a major Japanese army on the Asian mainland. The intellectual

Alanbrooke (1883–1963) was largely responsible for curbing Churchill's more madcap military projects. Fitness fanatic **Montgomery** (1887–1979) was a highly effective field commander in North Africa, Sicily, and France but his prima donna personality led him to clash repeatedly with his great rival, **George S. Patton**. Churchill characterized Montgomery as being "in defeat, unbeatable; in victory, unbearable." Note the two cap-badges, a typically calculated eccentricity, intended to make him instantly recognizable to the men under his command. Dwarfed by these larger-than-life figures stands an elegant, life-size bronze of pint-sized **Sir Walter Raleigh** (1552–1618) - poet and courtier, historian and herbalist, promoter of British colonization in America and of American tobacco in Britain. The statue was erected to mark the 350th anniversary of the settlement of Jamestown, Va. in 1607. Raleigh financed the ill-fated expedition to settle Roanoke island but Elizabeth I was too attached to him to let him risk his own life. The statue stands where Raleigh is supposed to have first met the Queen, in the Privy Garden of Whitehall Palace. Fearful James I was much less attached to Raleigh and imprisoned him in the Tower for 13 years for his alleged knowledge of a conspiracy against the throne. Then, after a futile voyage in search of South American gold which cost Raleigh his health and a son, James had him executed in Old Palace Yard (between the present Houses of Parliament and Westminster Abbey).

On the opposite side of Whitehall, guarded by black gates, is Downing St. No. 10 has been the official residence of the Prime Minister since 1735. No. 11 is occupied by the Chancellor of the Exchequer (the equivalent of the Minister of Finance) and No. 12 by the Chief Whip of the governing party (in charge of party discipline). The street takes its name from its developer, **Sir George Downing** (1623–84), a Harvard graduate, who returned to England during the Commonwealth (1649–60), initially to serve Cromwell by spying on Royalists, then switching sides to become a double agent. Diarist Samuel Pepys (1633–1703) dismissed him as "a perfidious rogue" but he evidently had his uses and in 1680 was rich enough to build this street on land leased from the Crown. Half a century later, after Downing's lease expired, it was rebuilt. Downing's childless grandson, another George, left his fortune to found Downing College, Cambridge. In 1785, **John Adams** (1735–1826), independent America's first diplomatic representative in London, came to No. 10 to meet Prime Minister **William Pitt the Younger** (1759–1806) to tie up the financial and other practical issues arising from American independence. Adams was not impressed by the youthful Pitt, who had become Prime Minister at the age of 24. During World War Two, CBS broadcaster **Edward R. Murrow** (1908–65) often came to No. 10 for a small hours drink with Prime Minister Winston Churchill (1874–1965), in the interval between Murrow's two nightly transmissions at 12:45 a.m. and 3:45 a.m.

The turning on the left, next after the Ministry of Defence building, is Richmond Terrace. This was once the home

The Houses of Parliament, viewed from St. Thomas's Hospital.

of **Henry Morton Stanley** (1841–1904), who shot to fame when he brought off the journalistic scoop of the nineteenth century by finding Scottish missionary-explorer David Livingstone, who had been "lost" for years in "darkest Africa." Welsh-born, illegitimate John Rowlands adopted the name Stanley after running away to sea and being adopted by a New Orleans merchant of that name. Stanley achieved the unusual distinction of fighting on both sides during the American Civil War. Captured as a Confederate at Shiloh, he enlisted in the U.S. Navy and after the war became a roving correspondent for the *New York Herald* in war-torn Crete and Ethiopia. Fame and fortune ultimately led Stanley to renounce his U.S. citizenship and revert to being British in order to serve as a Member of Parliament and accept a knighthood.

Continue along Whitehall into Parliament St. and then into Parliament Square to view the statues standing in the center island. **Churchill's** statue stands prominently at one corner; interestingly, he wears a greatcoat which might be either military (he was a cavalry officer as a young man) or naval (he was First Lord of the Admiralty, in charge of the navy, at the outbreak of both World Wars). Born the eldest son of Lord Randolph Churchill and American heiress Jenny Jerome, Churchill was the grandson of an English Duke and the American millionaire owner of the *New York Times* but, as he never went to university, thought of himself as a disadvantaged outsider in public life. Churchill visited the U.S. no less than 15 times and during World War Two addressed both the U.S. Congress and the Canadian Parliament in Ottawa, where a famous portrait was taken of him by Canadian photographer Yusef Karsh. Churchill's many honors included the Nobel Prize for Literature (1953) and the unique accolade of honorary U.S. citizenship, conferred by special Act of Congress at the initiative of President John F. Kennedy.

At Churchill's back stands South African statesman

Jan Smuts (1870–1950), sculpted by New York-born **Sir Jacob Epstein**. Next comes belligerent **Lord Palmerston** (1784–1865), who brought Britain and the U.S. to the brink of war in 1861, when Confederate emissaries aboard the British ship *Trent* were seized by force by a boarding-party from a Union warship; only the deathbed intervention of Queen Victoria's husband, Prince Albert, averted the crisis. In the corner stands **Lord Derby** (1799–1869). On the plinth of his statue a bronze plaque shows him chairing a committee to provide relief for Lancashire factory hands unemployed by the "cotton famine" caused by the Union blockade of the Confederacy. Despite their sufferings the working-classes remained firm supporters of the Union and Abolitionist cause. The upper classes, seeing Confederate grandees as fellow aristocrats, sympathized with the South. Thus Britain, divided, remained neutral. Beside Derby stands **Benjamin Disraeli** (1804–81), Britain's only Jewish Prime Minister, who designated a delighted Victoria "Empress of India," and secured the Suez Canal from Britain by borrowing £10,000,000 from Rothschilds on his personal say-so. In the furthest corner stands **Sir Robert Peel** (1788–1850), the first man to get a double First Class degree at Oxford and the founder of London's Metropolitan Police (hence "bobbies"). On the other side of the road stands Prime Minister **George Canning** (1770–1827), an ardent supporter of South American independence from Spanish rule, and next to him towers a huge **Abraham Lincoln** (1809–65). First proposed in 1914 by the "American Committee for the Celebration of the Hundredth Anniversary of Peace Among English-Speaking Peoples" (i.e., the ending of the War of 1812), the statue, a copy of the Chicago Lincoln Memorial by Irish-American Augustus Saint-Gaudens, was finally unveiled in 1920.

Cross the road to enter Westminster Abbey. Please remember that this is not a museum but an active

The coronation of Edward VII 1902. The royal procession approaches the west door of the Abbey. The buildings in the right foreground no longer exist.

church and that prayers will be said on the hour. No photography is permitted. Originally built by Edward the Confessor (reigned 1042–66), whose shrine now lies surrounded by a score of kings and queens, the present Abbey was reconstructed (first phase 1245–70) in the latest French style by Henry III (reigned 1216–72) but not finally completed until the imposing west towers (beneath which you enter) were finished five centuries later. For over nine centuries "*the* Abbey," as Londoners refer to it, has served as the setting for royal coronations and as a pantheon for the burial or commemoration of the great, the good, and the, by now, utterly obscure. The American physician and humorist **Oliver Wendell Holmes** (1809–94) referred to the Abbey unflatteringly as a "great museum of gigantic funereal bric-a-brac." Whatever. American visitors have been coming here since at least 1689, when it was on the itinerary of **Samuel Sewall**, the first transatlantic tourist to have left a detailed record of his visit. Confining a visit to the nave North American visitors may be especially interested in the following memorials:

Under the northwest Belfry Tower (immediately to your left as you enter) - **Viscount Howe** (1725-58) - "the best soldier in the British Army" - killed during an expedition to take the French-held Fort Ticonderoga. Massachusetts paid for the memorial, by **Scheemakers**, the foremost sculptor of his day, who also sculpted the Shakespeare which stands in Poets' Corner and Leicester Square. Howe is buried in St. Peter's, Albany, N.Y.

In the north aisle of the nave - **Charles James Fox** (1749-1806), radical, libertine, drunkard, gambler, and defender of the American Revolution. A grossly flattering memorial to a man of gross personal habits and great personal charm. Note the sorrowing black slave - a reference to his last public service, moving the bill to abolish slave-trading in the British Empire. Along the wall above is the Strathcona window, commemorating **Richard II** (1377-99) and **Abbot Litlyngton** who between them completed Henry III's work of reconstruction. **Baron Strathcona** (1820-1914) worked his way up from Hudson Bay Company apprentice to corporate chief, main financier of the Canadian Pacific Railway, president of the Bank of Montreal, and Canadian High Commissioner in London.

In the shadow of the next window to the east lies "Scientists' Corner." Alongside the graves or memorials of **Newton, Faraday, Darwin,** and **Kelvin,** New Zealand-born **Ernest Rutherford** (1871-1937) is honored. Professor of physics at McGill University, Montreal and then at Manchester and Cambridge, Rutherford's pioneering investigations laid the theoretical groundwork for the harnessing of atomic power and won him the Nobel prize (for chemistry!) in 1908.

The nave is dominated by the Grave of the Unknown Warrior, perpetually surrounded by poppies, the blood-red symbol of sacrifice. Nearby, on a column, hangs the Congressional Medal of Honor, presented by General Pershing in 1921. Between the Grave and the west door lies an incised marble tablet bearing the somewhat superfluous command: "Remember Winston Churchill." (Churchill is actually buried, in an entirely unspectacular grave, alongside his parents in the churchyard at Bladon, near Oxford.)

To the east of the Grave (i.e., going towards the gold, neo-Gothic screen) a tablet marks the temporary resting place of banker-philanthropist **George Peabody** (1795–1869) (see p. 69). Prior to the return of his body to his native Massachusetts aboard the newest and largest warship in the Royal Navy, Peabody gave £500,000 towards housing for London's poor and in effect invented the modern charitable foundation.

In the center of the nave lies the grave of **David Livingstone** (1813–73), the missionary-explorer "found" by H. M. Stanley in 1871; Livingstone's heart remained in Africa (literally!).

In the south aisle of the nave, at the easternmost end – **Andrew Bonar Law** (1858–1923), Canadian-born Prime Minister of Britain (1922–3). Born in New Brunswick of Scottish descent, Bonar Law became a Glasgow iron merchant before entering politics as a Conservative. Colleagues found him aloof and ultra-cautious. His premiership was curtailed by poor health. Former Liberal PM Asquith remarked after the interment of Law's ashes, "it is fitting that we should have buried the Unknown Prime Minister by the side of the Unknown Soldier." Nearby stands an imposing monument to a much more controversial figure, **Major John André** (1751–80). During the Revolutionary War André was sent secretly to General Benedict Arnold, who wanted to surrender West Point to the British. Intercepted by the rebels, André was sentenced to hang as a spy and denied his request for a soldier's death by firing squad. The news plunged the British army into mourning and enraged opinion in Britain. George III (reigned 1760–1820) personally arranged and paid for the monument, which shows Washington receiving André's vain petition, while above Britannia and a British lion recline in sorrow. Although André's body was returned forty years later after a respectful send-off, the entire incident aroused such passions on both sides that the heads of both Washington and André have been broken off the monument several times and two attempts to erect a memorial to André in the States have been violently thwarted by vandals.

At the west end of the aisle, backing onto St. George's Chapel, is a memorial to **Robert Baden-Powell** (1857–1941), war hero and founder of the worldwide Boy Scout movement.

Beside the doorway, on the west wall, a monument to **Franklin Delano Roosevelt** (1882–1945) acclaims him as "A faithful friend of freedom and of Britain."

(In the chapels beyond the nave (£) stand monuments to the youthful general **James Wolfe** (1727–59), conqueror of Quebec; explorer **Sir John Franklin** (1786–1847) whose entire expedition perished in the Canadian Arctic in a vain attempt to find a Northwest Passage to link the Atlantic and Pacific; and the second **Earl of Halifax** (1716–71), a promoter of Nova Scotia, after whom the port of Halifax is named. The dazzlingly refurbished Henry VII chapel, home of the Order of the Bath, contains a memorial plate bearing the arms of **Sir John A. Macdonald** (1815–91), Canada's first Prime Minister. Former President George Bush is also a holder of the Order of the Bath. Poets' Corner contains memorials to the American poet **Longfellow** (1807–82), to **T. S. Eliot** (1888–1965), an American who became British, and to **W. H. Auden** (1907–73), a Briton who became American. The striking bronze of the poet, engraver, and mystic **William Blake** (1757–1827) to be seen there is by Epstein.)

Leave the nave by the small doorway in the south aisle

to enter the north cloister. When the Abbey was a Benedictine monastery this cloister, which had the best light, was the scriptorium, where monks copied books and documents and taught their juniors how to write. Now it contains a modest memorial to **General John Burgoyne** (1722–92) who surrendered his 5,000 men to American rebel forces at Saratoga in 1777. That ended his military career but, undaunted, he turned to drama and wrote a hit play *The Heiress*. His gravestone was only positively identified in 1960.

Pass along past the brass-rubbers into the east cloister, to note the sketches depicting scenes from the Abbey's history. On the left is the entrance to the octagonal Chapter House (£), a superb example of medieval artistry and engineering in harmony, recognized as "incomparable" as soon as it was completed around 1250. Inside are memorials to poet and diplomat **James Russell Lowell** (1819–91) ("Placed here by his English friends") and ambassador **Walter Hines Page** (1855–1918) ("friend of Great Britain in her sorest need" - i.e., World War One).

Continue past the Pyx Chamber and Undercroft Museum down a passageway and left towards a delightful garden, framed by a charming archway. Yet another U.S. diplomat, the writer **Washington Irving** (1783–1859), stayed here for a happy month in 1842, mightily gratified by the warm reception he received from the young Queen Victoria and Prince Albert.

Retrace your footsteps and just past the Undercroft Museum, turn left into the south cloister and pause to look at a monument showing the routes and craft of three English circumnavigators of the globe. **Sir Francis Drake** (1540–96) returned with a fortune in Spanish gold, for which a grateful Elizabeth I (1558–1603) knighted him. His *Golden Hind* became a "visitor attraction" until it literally fell apart. Drake later rescued the first Virginian colonists from disaster, but whether he did actually touch California and claim it for the Queen, as the monument implies, is a matter of historical dispute. **Captain James Cook** (1728–79), although self-taught, was the most brilliant navigator of his day, mapping more of the earth's surface than anyone before or since. His surveys of the St. Lawrence made possible Wolfe's surprise capture of Quebec and gained him command of a Royal Society expedition to Tahiti to observe the transit of Venus. The ship depicted, *Endeavour*, was built as a coastal coal-carrier and derided by fellow-seamen as a clumsy tub but it, and another of his vessels, *Discovery*, inspired the names of U.S. space-rockets. Cook proved New Zealand was not part of Australia, which he claimed for Britain, and was the first voyager to enter Antarctic waters. With his assistant, George Vancouver, he also surveyed large sections of the northwest coast of North America, before being killed in Hawaii, trying to pacify a quarrel between local people and his crew. **Sir Francis Chichester** (1901–72) won the first solo transatlantic yacht race (1960) and then, after recovering from cancer, made the first single-handed circumnavigation of the world (1966–7), to be knighted by Elizabeth II with the same sword Elizabeth I used to knight Drake four centuries before. His *Gypsy Moth IV* can be seen at Greenwich, in the shadow of the clipper *Cutty Sark*.

Continue out of the south cloister into Dean's Yard. At the far end on the east side is the entrance to Westminster School, whose alumni include architect Sir Christopher Wren, philosopher John Locke, hymn-writer Charles Wesley, actor Peter Ustinov, and composer Sir Andrew Lloyd-Webber. The father of the original *Alice in Wonderland* was once headmaster here.

Turn right out of the neo-Gothic gateway and pause in front of the Abbey to note the Central Hall, which serves as headquarters to the Methodist Church. The first meetings of the newly-formed United Nations were held here in 1945.

Continue along the pathway running through the railed

Oliver Cromwell, Westminster Hall, and Big Ben.

green beside the Abbey and enter the church of St. Margaret's, Westminster, which serves as the parish church of the House of Commons and has long been fashionable for weddings. Milton, Pepys, Bentham, and Churchill were all married here. A brass plate claims it as the burial-place of Sir Walter Raleigh (possibly). There is also a memorial window to Raleigh, with a tribute composed by James Russell Lowell, and another to Milton, with a tribute by John Greenleaf Whittier.

Leave by the east door and cross the road to pause by the statue of **Oliver Cromwell** (1599–1658), executioner of Charles I, with one hand on his sword and the other clutching the Bible.

Look back across the road and note that someone with a quirky sense of humor has placed a cast of the monarch's severed head above a doorway, so that the Lord

The Embankment from Hungerford Bridge. The Hotel Cecil (first building on the left) was, with 800 rooms, the largest hotel in Europe when it opened in 1886. In 1931 the river side was refronted when it was converted to become Shell-Mex House.

Protector can admire his handiwork. Behind Cromwell is Westminster Hall, the only part of the Old Palace of Westminster to survive the catastrophic fire of 1834. Built in the reign of William II (reigned 1087–1100), it was rebuilt in the fourteenth century and has accommodated the Law Courts (until 1882), the trial of Charles I, the coronation banquet of George III, and the lying-in-state of Winston Churchill.

Head eastwards past Churchill's statue, cross the road at the traffic lights and turn right towards the river to Westminster station (Circle and District lines). Walk ends.

En Route: Richard Recommends

Food and Drink

Villiers St. has a dozen different kinds of food outlets and on the south side of Trafalgar Sq./north end of Whitehall are numerous tourist-oriented pubs and restaurants. Excellent coffee at Westminster Abbey.

Victorian period pubs include the Sherlock Holmes (Northumberland St., off Northumberland Ave.), the Red Lion (Whitehall), and the Albert (Victoria St., about 400 yards west of Westminster Abbey).

Public Toilets

Victoria Embankment Gardens (just east of Embankment station). Parliament St. (underpass, £). Storey's Gate (opposite side of the road from Westminster Abbey, tucked away underground, £). Westminster Pier (in the wall of the embankment).

Delays and Diversions

Brass-rubbing at Westminster Abbey. Make your own souvenir of medieval England (£; all materials supplied). Allow at least half an hour.

Cabinet War Rooms at the junction of King Charles St. and Horse Guards Rd. Churchill's bomb-proof bunker, complete with "hot-line" to FDR. Allow an hour.

Shopping and Souvenirs

The Parliamentary Bookshop at the corner of Parliament St. and Bridge St. has posters, pamphlets, and books for politics buffs. Westminster Abbey's shop has quality souvenirs, books and CDs/tapes of its choir. The National Trust shop at Caxton St., off Buckingham Gate, is housed in a stunning 18th-century charity school and has a splendid selection of classy gifts reflecting classic English lifestyles; ideal for one-stop shopping. Immediately opposite is a first-class specialist map shop. Artillery Row (opposite side of Victoria St. from Buckingham Gate) has Whittard's, selling bizarre teapots.

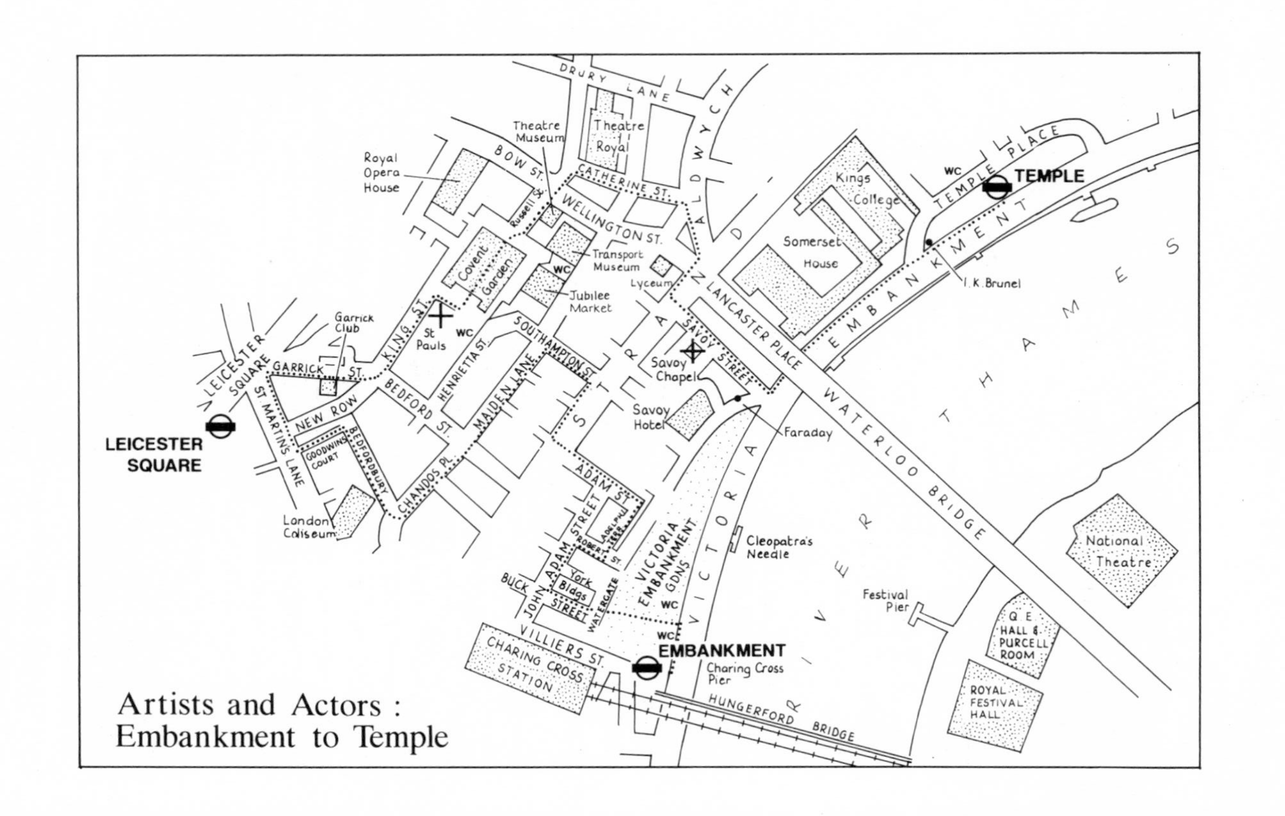

Artists and Actors : Embankment to Temple

2

Artists and Actors: Embankment to Temple

This is a walk of twists and turns, where you never know what's just around the next corner. It takes in both elegant residential streets three centuries old, the cheerful chaos of Covent Garden market, and sections of London's Theatreland. And, if you're keen to be diverted for eating or shopping, this itinerary is for *you*.

Starting Point - Embankment station (Circle or District lines)
Turn right out of the ticket-barriers to emerge onto the Thames Embankment, with Hungerford foot- and railway-bridge to your right. Across the river loom the Royal Festival Hall and the National Theatre. On the opposite side of the road, on the wall of the Thames Embankment, note a monument to librettist **W. S. Gilbert**, the Gilbert of "Gilbert and Sullivan." Their "Savoy Operas" have enjoyed a century of huge success on both sides of the Atlantic, with professional and amateur companies. Gilbert could never bring himself to watch a first night and would pace this stretch of the Embankment until he could hear the final applause roll out from the nearby Savoy theater - hence the otherwise eccentric location of this monument. Cole Porter (who composed a Gilbert and Sullivan parody when he was only ten) and Ira Gershwin both acknowledged Gilbert's witty ditties as a major inspiration for their own work.

Turn left and left again into Victoria Embankment Gardens and over to your right see a romantic statue of

Robert Burns (1759–96), a smaller version of one previously erected in New York's Central Park. "Auld Lang Syne" is the best-known work of Scotland's national poet but he is shown holding a manuscript of "To Mary in Heaven," addressed to a dead lover. Novelist **George Orwell** (1903–50) "slept rough" in these gardens around 1930 when, living as a tramp, he was collecting material for his first published book, *Down and Out in Paris and London.*

Leave the gardens to pass through the right hand side of a Watergate which also has associations with a politically controversial figure. In the 1620s, this was the waterside entrance to the splendid London home of vain, stylish, pushy **George Villiers**, Duke of Buckingham (1592–1628), upon whom both James I and Charles I showered favors, money, and offices before, to general satisfaction, an assassin brought an abrupt end to his career of almost unparalleled diplomatic and military bungling.

Walk up the steps into Buckingham St., where at No. 14 and the house next door **Samuel Pepys** lived in retirement with his fine library, after his brilliant career as a naval administrator was cut short by political intrigues arising from his loyalty to the Catholic Duke of York. Two centuries later No. 14 was occupied by American artist **Joseph Pennell** (1857–1926) and his wife **Elizabeth** (1855–1936), keen admirers of **J. A. M. Whistler** (1834–1903), who was a frequent attender at their "open house" Thursday evenings. Two years after their hero's death Joseph organized a massive (1,000 exhibits) Whistler Memorial Exhibition which was opened by Rodin. The Pennells then wrote the first major biography of Whistler.

Continue up Buckingham St., noting the fine eighteenth-century doorways on Nos. 13 and 18, and turn right into John Adam St., which, with its neighbors, commemorates the Scottish **Adam** brothers, whose mastery of neo-Classical architecture and design enabled them to take London by storm in the mid-eighteenth century. Alas, they overstretched themselves with the majestic Adelphi (from the Greek for "brothers"), an immense apartment complex which stood here overlooking the Thames until its senseless demolition in 1936. But on the north side of John Adam St. their headquarters building for the Royal Society of Arts (1772–4) still stands at No. 8. No. 6 was formerly the Adelphi Family Hotel, where **Abigail Adams** lodged in 1784 "as quiet as at any place in Boston." London she thought expensive but "pleasanter than I expected . . . and more sunshine than I thought to have found." By the time **James Fenimore Cooper** stayed there in 1828, the hotel was known as Wright's. He had come intending to write a belligerent book, refuting supposed British prejudices against Americans. But *The Last of the Mohicans* had already made him famous and admired and so, as his wife recorded, "the Johnny Bulls are so civil to him that I am afraid he will not be able to abuse them, and so the piquancy of his book will be quite spoiled." When strolling street musicians played "Yankee Doodle" outside his window he was at least consoled with the thought that "it is something, at all events, to have taught John Bull that we take pride in that tune."

Opposite the first turning on the right, York Buildings, a blue plaque commemorates caricaturist **Thomas Rowlandson** (1757–1827), a brilliant draftsman whose work is now considered highly collectible. York Buildings was where the American painters **Gilbert Stuart** (1755–1828) and **John Trumbull** (1756–1843) lodged, in 1775 and 1780 respectively. Stuart, a Loyalist who had abandoned Rhode Island for Nova Scotia, nevertheless returned to the States in 1792 and painted over a thousand portraits, including Washington and Jefferson. Trumbull, an ex-colonel in the Revolutionary army, came with a letter of introduction from Benjamin Franklin, trusting to an amnesty proclaimed for ex-rebels. Unfortunately the furor after the hanging of

Major André (see p. 13) led to Trumbull's arrest. He used his imprisonment to finish a painting of St. Jerome (now in Yale University Art Gallery) and make nude sketches of a fellow male prisoner (now owned by Fordham University, New York). Trumbull was released after his fellow artists and countrymen Benjamin West (1738–1820) and John Singleton Copley (1738–1815) put up £400 bail. Not a man to bear a grudge, he later returned to resume training under West, returned again as secretary to John Jay at the American embassy, and even took an English wife. Trumbull is chiefly remembered for large-scale compositions of such stirring events as the battle of Bunker's Hill, the Declaration of Independence, and the British surrenders at Saratoga and Yorktown. Most of his works, reproduced in generations of American history textbooks, are in the Trumbull Gallery at Yale.

Take the second turning right into Robert St. (named for the oldest Adam brother) and pause outside Nos. 1–3, once the home of **Robert Adam** (1728–92) and later of poet **Thomas Hood** (1799–1845), **John Galsworthy** (1867–1933), author of the *Forsyte Saga* and winner of the 1932 Nobel Prize for Literature, and of **Sir James Barrie** (1860–1937), creator of *Peter Pan*. (The model for the statue of Peter Pan which stands in Kensington Gardens was the *44-year-old* actress Nina Boucicault, daughter of the Irish-American actor-playwright Dion Boucicault (1822–90).)

Turn left in front of the 1938 office block which occupies the Adelphi site, pass along Adelphi Terrace and under the covered passageway and pause to note on the easternmost column an inscription recording the names of distinguished former residents and institutions – two friends of **Dr. Samuel "Dictionary" Johnson** (1709–84), bibliophile **Topham Beauclerk** and actor-manager **David Garrick** (1717–79); impresario **Richard D'Oyly-Carte** (1844–1901), who produced the Savoy Operas and sent Oscar Wilde to lecture on aesthetics in the Wild West; novelist **Thomas Hardy** (1840–1928), who trained here as an architect under Arthur Blomfield; playwright **George Bernard Shaw**; the London School of Economics, established by Shaw's socialist friends, Sidney and Beatrice Webb; and the Savage Club, of which Mark Twain was an honorary member.

Looking towards the Thames you should be able to catch a glimpse of "Cleopatra's Needle," an Egyptian obelisk (*c.*1475 BC) erected here in 1878.

A tram passes Cleopatra's Needle. Trams went out of service in London in 1952. The electric lighting along the Embankment is London's oldest, dating from the 1880s, and drawing power from London's first power station, which was installed by Thomas Edison.

Turn left up Adam St. and pause outside Nos. 1–5, where a plaque marks the former offices of the Company which began the organized British settlement of New Zealand in 1840 *and pause again outside* No. 8, an original Adam house and former home of pioneer industrialist **Sir Richard Arkwright** (1732–92), who almost certainly purloined the secret of the cotton-spinning machine which made his fortune.

Turn right into the Strand, cross it, turn left into Southampton St. and then left into Maiden Lane. Poet **Andrew Marvell** lived at No. 9 in 1677, **Voltaire** lodged at No. 9 in 1727–8, and England's greatest painter, **J. M. W. Turner** (1775–1851) was born here, above his father's barber shop at No. 26, which is still a barber's. Rule's claims (plausibly) to be the capital's oldest restaurant. Dickens certainly dined there and so did Edward VII, with his mistress, actress Lillie Langtry (1852–1929), who was a huge success in the U.S. and allegedly the life's love of the legendary Judge Roy Bean.

Continue into Chandos Place, pausing at the junction with Bedford St. to glance up and note a plaque marking the site of the shoe-blacking factory where **Dickens** spent a traumatic six months as a teenager while his father was imprisoned in the Marshalsea for debt (see p. 87). The experience left him with a lifelong sympathy for exploited children, who occur as a motif throughout his novels.

At the end of Chandos Place turn right into Bedfordbury and note on the right Duval Court, a new Peabody Estate block which still incorporates the distinctive horizontal colored brick banding which has long been characteristic of Peabody buildings. *Just before the top, on the left, pass through* Goodwin's Court, a rare and truly Dickensian passageway dating from 1690, *to emerge into* theater-lined St. Martin's Lane, once home to London's main art school, which trained Hogarth, Kent, Gainsborough, and West, until it merged with the Royal Academy in 1768. Ohio-born **Charles Frohman**

(1860–1915), friend of Mark Twain and the Boucicaults, father and son, managed the Duke of York's Theatre (left) here from 1897 until his death aboard the *Lusitania*, torpedoed by a German U-boat. Frohman gave *Peter Pan* its debüt in 1904. The Albery Theatre (right), founded in 1903 as the New Theatre, was managed by the younger **Dion Boucicault** and premiered Shaw's *St. Joan* (1924) and T. S. Eliot's *The Cocktail Party* (1950).

Turn right, passing a plaque marking the site (No. 61) of **Thomas Chippendale's** furniture workshop (1753–1813), and *go right into Garrick St.*, named for Dr. Johnson's pupil, protégé, and friend, who revived and purified productions of Shakespeare, founded Stratford-upon-Avon's Shakespeare Festival, and made a huge fortune. The gloomy-looking Garrick Club on the right was established in 1831 as a meeting-place for "actors and men of education and refinement." Past members have included Sir Henry Irving, Charles Dickens, Thackeray, Trollope, and W. S. Gilbert.

At the end of Garrick St. turn left into King St., and, passing on the left-hand side a plaque (on No. 32) to **Thomas Arne** (1710–78) composer of "Rule, Britannia," *enter Covent Garden and turn right to pause beneath* the portico of St. Paul's church, built by Inigo Jones in 1631–8 and appropriately renowned as "the Actors' church." An inscription on the wall records that Samuel Pepys saw the first Punch and Judy puppet show in England here in 1662. And it was in this porch that Professor Higgins and Colonel Pickering first encounter flower-seller Eliza Doolittle in the opening scene of Shaw's *Pygmalion*, which translated to the screen as *My Fair Lady*. Philadelphia-born tragedian **Edwin Forrest** (1806–72) married Catherine Sinclair here in 1837 against the wishes of her father. Ten years after the fairy-tale wedding, attended by U.S. minister **Andrew Stevens** and banker **Joshua Bates** (see pp. 105–6), the couple divorced after a sensational hearing in which each accused the other of flagrant infidelities. By then For-

When the Duke of Bedford asked Inigo Jones to build him a simple church much like a barn, the architect promised him "the handsomest barn in England." Now street entertainers perform underneath the massive portico of St. Paul's, Covent Garden.

rest was immersed in a hugely destructive rivalry with English actor William Charles Macready (1793–1873), which culminated in tragedy in 1849 when a pro-Forrest mob attacked the Astor Place Opera House in New York City, where Macready was playing, and was fired on by militia, who killed 22 of the rioters.

Pass through the handsome market buildings, dating from the 1820s, and pause on the far side in Russell St. To the north, on your left, rears up the great bulk of the Royal Opera House. Pittsburgh-born soprano **Louise Homer** (1871–1947) triumphed here in 1899, attracting the patronage of the great Australian diva, Dame Nellie Melba, and being invited to sing for the Queen at Windsor. In 1919, it was here that Ohio-born journalist **Lowell Thomas** (1892–1981), assisted by a youthful public speaking teacher, **Dale Carnegie** (1888–1955), gave his spectacular two-hour presentation, complete with movie film and the band of the Welsh Guards, *The Last Crusade* – i.e., the adventures of (T. E.) "Lawrence of Arabia" (1888–1935). Thomas went on to a brilliant career in radio and TV broadcasting, Carnegie to make a fortune out of his bestseller *How to Win Friends and Influence People* (1936).

On the south side of Russell St., appropriately above Café Valerie, a blue plaque marks the site of Davies' bookshop where **Dr. Johnson** first met his future biographer **James Boswell** (1740–95), who apologized for being a Scot and let himself in for twenty years of teasing on that score.

Cross Bow St., turn right into Catherine St. and pause outside the Theatre Royal, Drury Lane. A theater has stood here since 1663, though the present, fourth, incarnation dates from 1812. Charles II's future mistress **Nell Gwynne** made her debut here to become the first great comedienne of the English stage. Under Garrick's management it became famous for Shakespeare. **Edwin Forrest** starred here as *Spartacus*. In the post-war period it has been the London home of lavish American musicals such as *Oklahoma* (1947), *Carousel* (1950), *South Pacific* (1951), *The King and I* (1953), *My Fair Lady* (1958), *Hello Dolly* (1965), and *Mame* (1969).

At the bottom of Catherine St. turn right into Aldwych, then cross Wellington St., pausing to spare a glance at the Lyceum, once **Sir Henry Irving's** (1838–1905) theater, where the great man played Othello to the Iago of **Edwin Booth** (1833–93), *then cross the Strand and go down* Savoy St. To the right stands the Savoy Chapel (1510) and beyond it the Savoy Hotel, established in 1884 by **Richard D'Oyly-Carte**, next to the Savoy Theatre he built to stage the Gilbert and Sullivan "Savoy Operas." (**Paul Robeson** made a brilliant debut there as Othello in 1930.) Carte had stayed in American luxury hotels and thought London badly needed something on the same lines but, when he announced his intention to install seventy bathrooms, his builder asked if he expected his guests to be amphibious. The first manager was César Ritz (see p. 158) and the first chef the great **Escoffier** (1846–1935), who created Peach Melba and Melba toast to honor Dame Nellie. Between them they pioneered the use of a data-base to record guests' whims. **Monet** stayed here to paint Thames fogs from the fifth floor. In 1914 future U.S. President (1929–33) **Herbert Hoover** (1874–1964), then a London-based mining engineer, set up a rent-free office here to repatriate 120,000 Americans stranded in Europe by the outbreak of World War One. The Savoy has remained a favorite with generations of Americans, including **Laurel and Hardy, Jimmy Durante, Errol Flynn, Clark Gable, James Stewart, Bob Hope, Bing Crosby, Danny Kaye, and John Wayne.**

At the bottom of Savoy St. pause to note the statue of **Michael Faraday** (1791–1867), pioneer of electricity, whose portrait adorns the £20 note. Appropriately, he stands outside the Institute of Electrical Engineers, which, in the 1920s, was the home of the BBC.

Turn left under Waterloo Bridge and walk past the former riverside frontage of Somerset House and King's College. Pause at the junction with Temple Place to note the statue of **Isambard Kingdom Brunel** (1806–59), engineer of the Great Western Railway (London–Bristol) and creator of *SS Great Britain*, the first all-iron, all-steam ship to cross the Atlantic. Brunel's jinxed masterpiece, the mammoth *Great Eastern*, laid the transatlantic cable which joined Britain and the U.S. by telegraph from 1866 onwards.

Continue along the Embankment to reach Temple station (Circle and District lines) on your left. Walk ends.

En route: Richard Recommends

Food and Drink

Once you get to the Strand there are over eighty pubs, cafés, or restaurants actually along this route or immediately visible from it. The short stretch of Maiden Lane

Eliza Doolittle must be there somewhere . . . The Flower Market at Covent Garden *c.* 1903. Shaw's *Pygmalion* was premiered in London in 1916, *My Fair Lady* in 1957.

alone has Rule's (classic English), a Greek taverna, a Canadian and an Australian bar, Fat Boy's Diner and a Mongolian barbecue, as well as regular pubs. King St. has the Calabash restaurant at the Africa Centre, the Canadian Muffin Co., and Sheila's (Australian). Other options en route include Italian, Indian, French, and Thai.

Public Toilets

Victoria Embankment (east of Embankment station). Henrietta St. (SW corner of Covent Garden). Jubilee Market (S side of Covent Garden).

Delays and Diversions

St. Paul's Church, Covent Garden. (Entrance through passages in King St. and Henrietta St.) Dozens of memorials to the greats of stage and screen - **Charlie Chaplin, Noel Coward, Vivien Leigh, William Henry**

Pratt (Boris Karloff!). Quiet churchyard, ideal for a discreet picnic.

London Transport Museum, Covent Garden. "Hands-on" history of buses, trams, taxis, trains, etc.

Museum of Theatre History, Russell St. Includes opera and ballet.

Shopping and Souvenirs

Covent Garden is a shop-till-you-drop honeycomb of specialist outlets: The Irish Shop (King St.), Penhaligons (fragrances, Wellington St.), Hackett's, Moss Bros. (traditionally pronounced "Moss Bross") (men's formal wear, King St.), Arthur Middleton (antique scientific instruments, New Row), Gamba (ballet shoes, dance wear). Jubilee market (S side of Covent Garden) has "craft" and "ethnic" goods, T-shirts, etc., while Cecil Court (off St. Martin's Lane) offers antique, prints, maps, coins, and bookshops specializing in dance and travel. The Transport and Theatre Museums both have shops selling posters, books, and souvenirs. In the market buildings themselves are sellers of kitchenware, doll's houses, avant-garde fashion, historical souvenirs, toy theaters, etc. etc.

3

Word Power: Temple to Blackfriars

The overriding theme of this walk is words and their power. The area it passes through has been associated for centuries with lawyers, journalists, publishers, and printers. It also includes three churches and a pub with strong North American associations, as well as two stops essential for anyone interested in tracing their family history.

Starting Point - Temple station (Circle/District lines)
Turn left out of the station and then left into Victoria Embankment Gardens. The statues here are a high-minded bunch. **W. E. Forster** was a pioneer of mass elementary education, **Lady Somerset** a temperance campaigner, and **John Stuart Mill** the leading liberal philosopher and economist of the nineteenth century and an early advocate of women's rights.

Exit to face a striking Gothic building, the former Astor Estate Office, on the opposite side of the road. **William Waldorf Astor** (1848–1919), super-rich and super-snob, despairing of the rising tide of democracy in America, fled to England in 1890 as "a country fit for gentlemen to live in." Equating wealth with status was, however, a cardinal error in the British context and indisputable proof of vulgarity, as Astor was to discover. He bought a handsome Buckinghamshire residence, Cliveden, and also a clutch of publications, including *The Observer*, a leading Sunday newspaper, led by **J. L. Garvin** (1868–1947), arguably the greatest journalist of the day.

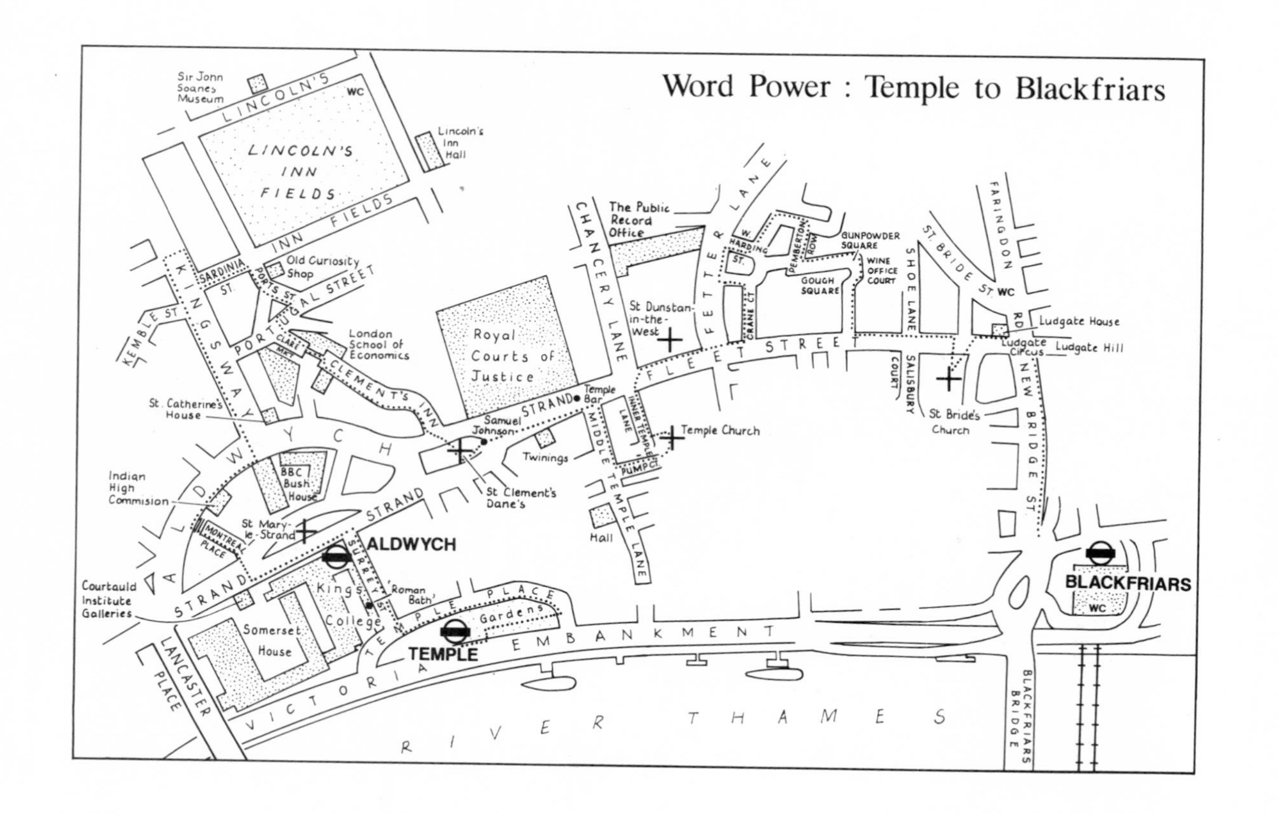
Word Power : Temple to Blackfriars
Sir John Soanes Museum
LINCOLN'S
WC
LINCOLN'S INN FIELDS
INN FIELDS
Lincoln's Inn Hall
SARDINIA ST.
Old Curiosity Shop
PORTS ST.
PORTUGAL STREET
KEMBLE ST
KINGSWAY
CLARE MKT
London School of Economics
CLEMENT'S INN
Royal Courts of Justice
St. Catherine's House
ALDWYCH
BBC Bush House
Indian High Commision
St Mary-le-Strand
MONTREAL PLACE
STRAND
ALDWYCH
Courtauld Institute Galleries
Somerset House
Kings College
SURREY ST
'Roman Bath'
TEMPLE PLACE
Gardens
TEMPLE
LANCASTER PLACE
VICTORIA EMBANKMENT
RIVER THAMES
Samuel Johnson
St Clement's Dane's
Twinings
Temple Bar
CHANCERY LANE
The Public Record Office
St Dunstan-in-the-West
FETTER LANE
W. HARDING ST.
PEMBERTON ROW
CRANE CT
GOUGH SQUARE
GUNPOWDER SQUARE
WINE OFFICE COURT
FLEET STREET
INNER TEMPLE LANE
MIDDLE TEMPLE LANE
PUMP CT
Temple Church
Hall
SHOE LANE
SALISBURY COURT
St Bride's Church
ST. BRIDE ST.
FARINGDON RD
Ludgate House
Ludgate Circus
Ludgate Hill
NEW BRIDGE ST.
BLACKFRIARS
BLACKFRIARS BRIDGE

Waldorf Astor's estate office, surmounted by its "Santa Maria" weather vane.

Astor's mock-medieval baronial hall was built in 1895 to enable him to keep a proprietorial eye on his print empire. Its aged architect, **John Loughborough Pearson** (1817–97), actually specialized in designing imposing churches but instinctively understood that what Astor really wanted was not an efficient setting for the conduct of business but a holy of holies to which lesser mortals could be summoned to be impressed by the opulence and taste of their employer. No unnecessary expense was spared. Professor Pevsner compliments the result – perhaps tongue in cheek – as "a perfect gem of its kind." Built entirely of highly durable Portland stone, "Astor House," as it became known, sports a gleaming weather vane in the shape of Columbus's "Santa Maria." Astor adopted British citizenship in 1899 and, undeterred by the snubs of high society, gamely battered away at its portals by donating lavishly to colleges and charities. The outbreak of World War One in 1914 must have seemed a heaven-sent opportunity to give even more to the rash of new funds which sprang up to succor refugees, the maimed, and the bereaved. Astor gave and gave - and, in 1916, at long last *received*, becoming "Baron Astor of Hever Castle in the County of Kent" and thus the first American-born member of the House of Lords. Fate denied him a suitably aristocratic demise. He died, just three years later, locked in the lavatory of a house in Brighton.

Retrace your steps along Temple Place and, opposite a green, wooden hut for cab-drivers, turn right up Surrey Street, then left into the Strand, passing King's College and pause outside Somerset House. Designed by **Sir William Chambers** in 1776 as the first purpose-built range of British government buildings, Somerset House now also houses the Courtauld Institute's world-class collection of Impressionist and Old Master paintings. In the courtyard stands an elaborately allegorical statue of prosaic but cultured **George III**, who encouraged the founding of the Royal Academy, which had its first proper home here.

Cross the Strand at the zebra crossing at the west end of James Gibbs' Italianate church of St. Mary-le-Strand (1717) and enter Montreal Place, where there is a bust of **Pandit Jawaharlal Nehru** (1889–1964), first Prime Minister of independent India, who attended Churchill's alma mater, Harrow.

Go up the steps and turn right past the elephant-embellished entrance to the Indian High Commission and pause when you see, at sidewalk level, an eroded but still legible memorial stone, recording the former site of the YMCA's "Eagle Hut," a temporary refuge for World War One doughboys desperately seeking doughnuts and drinkable coffee.

Cross the road into Kingsway (left, west side) and turn back to look at Bush House. Famed as the home of the BBC World Service, this imposing complex is not named to compliment the 41st President of the United

States but another American, businessman Irving T. Bush, who built it between 1925 and 1935 as a trade exhibition hall. The architects, **Helmle** and **Corbett**, were also American. At the top of the entrance archway two muscular figures, representing Britain and America, affirm their comradeship over a motto celebrating the friendship of English-speaking peoples; entitled *Youth*, this is the work of American sculptor **Malvina Hoffmann** (1887–1966). Note also, on the opposite corner of Kingsway, St. Catherine's House, where generations of Americans and Canadians have tracked their ancestries through its vast archive of records of births, marriages, and deaths.

Continue north along Kingsway and pause at Kemble Street, on your left, to view the bold brick blocks of the Wild Street Estate, with their trademark horizontal bands of striping, yet another testimony to the generosity of George Peabody.

At the next block north cross the road at the traffic lights and, on the opposite side of Kingsway, pause to look back at the building you have just passed, No. 65, which is notable for its early date – 1911. Its Scottish architect, **Sir John Burnet** (1857–1938), made a special tour of the United States to study the latest steel-framed office buildings, before finalizing his design. A state-of-the-art building, it was originally built as the London headquarters of an American company based on state-of-the-art technology – Kodak.

Walk south (back towards Bush House) and turn left into Sardinia Street. Pause at the corner of Lincoln's Inn Fields and look left to see the projecting entrance to Nos. 57–58, a Palladian house of 1730 and for many years the home of **John Forster**, the friend and biographer of Dickens. **Ralph Waldo Emerson** (1803–82) had dinner here on April 25, 1848 with **Dickens** and historian **Thomas Carlyle** (1795–1881), with whom he corresponded for forty years. As there were no ladies present "the conversation turned on the shameful lewdness of the London

57–58 Lincoln's Inn Field was the home of Dickens' friend and first biographer, John Forster, who entertained Emerson, Carlyle, and Dickens to dinner here. Dickens used the house as a model for the home of the lawyer Tulkinghorn in *Bleak House* – "formerly a house of state . . . let off in sets of chambers now; and in those broken fragments of greatness lawyers lie like maggots in nuts."

streets at night." Emerson assured the company that in America educated young men "go virgins to their nuptial bed, as truly as their brides." Dickens opined that, if that were to be true of one of his own sons, he would be worried for his health. The north side of Lincoln's Inn Fields is known as Canada Walk, in commemoration of its occupancy during World War Two by the headquarters of the Royal Canadian Air Force.

Turn right into Portsmouth Street and pause by "The Old Curiosity Shop," long sought out by generations of transatlantic literary pilgrims. The sign proclaims that it was immortalized by Dickens but, whichever ancient emporium the author had in mind as the home of Little Nell, it was not this one, though it may well be the oldest shop in London.

Turn right into Portugal Street and left into Clare Market. On either side stand the buildings of the London School of Economics and Political Science. **J. F. Kennedy** was briefly enrolled here as a student when his father was a (deeply unpopular) U.S. ambassador to Britain. The onset of war sent him home after barely a month. **Mick Jagger** was also a student at the LSE but dropped out to form the Rolling Stones.

Continue forward and pass through Clement's Inn Passage into Clement's Inn and pause to note a plaque on the right-hand side recording the former headquarters of the Women's Social and Political Union, founded in 1903 to agitate for female suffrage. One of its leading lights was American **Zelie Emerson**, who was arrested twice for her protests, served two months at hard labor and was beaten so severely by police during a suffragette demonstration that she was forced to return to the States.

At the bottom of Clement's Inn cross the Strand to enter St. Clement Dane's, the church of the Royal Air Force, rebuilt by Sir Christopher Wren in 1680–2 and totally gutted during the Blitz. The wall at the northwest corner of the nave houses a monument to the USAF, surrounded by a quotation from the Gettysburg address. The floor is decorated with plaques of squadron badges, including 29 Canadian ones (center aisle and front-left and front-right of it). The wall panels around the altar bear the names of three Canadian aces of World War One who won the Victoria Cross. **"Billy" Bishop** shot down 72 enemy planes in aerial combat but won his VC for a raid deep into enemy territory, in the course of which he destroyed an entire German squadron before it could even take off. **William George Barker**, despite being wounded three times, shot down five opponents

The Royal Courts of Justice.

and survived a crash landing. **Alan Arnett McLeod**, wounded in five places, landed his burning machine and dragged his even more severely wounded observer from the wreckage under enemy fire. He was nineteen. After a hero's welcome in Canada, he died five days before the end of the war - from influenza.

Cross back over the Strand to enter the Royal Courts of Justice. (Note: cameras are strictly banned from the precincts. The newspaper-seller nearby will usually mind them for a small charge.) The lofty and impressive Great Hall contains a statue of **Sir William Blackstone** (1723–80), whose massive *Commentaries on the Laws of England* exerted a fundamental influence on the drafting of the Constitution of the United States and on the subsequent development of the American legal system. Fittingly, the statue was the gift of the American Bar Association to mark the bicentenary of Blackstone's birth. To the right hangs a portrait of **Baron Lyndhurst** (1772–1863), Boston-born son of painter John Singleton Copley, who served no less than three times as Lord Chancellor. Asked if he believed in the possibility of platonic friendship between men and women, Lyndhurst knowingly replied, “After, but not before.” A small plaque on the wall to the right of the archway on the left records the unique facility afforded to U.S. servicemen during World War One of being allowed to bed down here for the night. The statue near the entrance is of **G. E. Street** (1824–81), whose exertions in building this mighty pile brought him to an early grave.

Once outside, turn back and look up to note that the entrance is surmounted by a statue of Christ, flanked by two other law-givers, Solomon and Alfred the Great, King of Wessex (871–899).

On leaving the Courts cross halfway over the Strand to pause by the statue of **Dr. Samuel Johnson**, a regular worshipper at St. Clement Dane’s. Dictating to six secretaries, Johnson single-handedly conceived and composed the first true dictionary of the English language, which, after six years of labor, was published in 1755 to huge acclaim. Thanks to the assiduous **James Boswell** (1740–1795), whose *Life* of Johnson is the first great literary biography, many of his conversational gems survived to make him the second most quoted Englishman after Shakespeare.

Continue across the road past the George (George III again!) to Twining’s shop, which has been selling tea here since 1706. Johnson, who was so addicted to tea that he feared for his health, would certainly have been a customer here.

Continue eastwards and pause to examine the print-filled windows of the Wig and Pen club, named for the lawyers and journalists who have long provided its custom. Among the prints you should find those of **Horace** (“Go west, young man!”) **Greeley** (1811–72), founder-editor of the *New York Tribune*, and of **Ulysses S. Grant** (1822–5), who, in 1877, became the first American President to visit Britain, where he received a tumultuous welcome. *The Times* rashly predicted that "after Washington, General Grant is the president who will occupy the largest place in the history of the United States."

Walk on and pass Temple Bar, an obelisk, surmounted by an heraldic dragon, marking the boundary between the City of Westminster and the City of London. Fleet Street, the "Street of Ink" (also "Street of Shame") has been a home to printers, publishers, and journalists for five centuries. Around 1900 it housed the editorial headquarters of almost six hundred publications. Even in 1980 there were half a dozen major newspapers located here. Now the whole industry has virtually

Dr. Samuel Johnson outside St. Clement Dane's, the church in which he worshipped.

vanished, dispersed to new, purpose-built facilities capable of housing the latest printing technologies.

Turn right through an archway of 1684 into Middle Temple Lane. Of the four Inns of Court which provide professional training for barristers (courtroom lawyers) and house the offices of the most prestigious law firms, Middle Temple has the strongest American links. Like many ambitious young men of Elizabethan times, both **Raleigh** and **Drake** passed terms here, not with any serious intention of becoming advocates, but because a smattering of law was useful to any gentleman, who would inevitably serve as a Justice of the Peace and be involved in family wrangles over wills and estate boundaries. Stately Middle Temple Hall (1573), which boasts a spectacular double hammerbeam roof, would certainly have been known to them. On February 2, 1602, Shakespeare himself is said to have taken part in the premiere of *Twelfth Night*, staged here in the presence of Elizabeth I. In the eighteenth century dozens of Americans, especially from Virginia and South Carolina, studied here, including six signers of the Declaration of Independence. Note the lists of names painted in the doorways, indicating seniority in each set of "chambers."

Pass through Pump Court and the Cloisters to reach the ancient (1185) Temple Church, one of only five circular churches in the entire country.

Walk up Inner Temple Lane to re-enter Fleet Street. Turn to look back above the archway at half-timbered Prince Henry's Room (1610), originally the Prince's Tavern, which now houses a small museum devoted to Samuel Pepys. Note the carving of the Prince of Wales's badge of three ostrich feathers, which also appears on the 2p piece.

Cross the road. (If you have a passion for family history and historical documents you may wish to divert a couple of hundred yards up Chancery Lane to the Public Record Office (right hand side. No charge).)

Continue east past Coutts, the royal bankers (hence the crowns on their sign). *On the opposite side of Fleet St. you can see* the Cock Tavern (which for most of its long existence stood on this side of the road!) where **T. S. Eliot** used to hold editorial meetings.

Continue east and stop outside the church of St. Dunstan-in-the-West. The heads either side of the entrance are those of **William Tyndale** (1494–1536) and **John Donne** (1572–1631), both of whom served this church. Tyndale made the first English translation of the entire Bible in a style so clear that he hoped it could be read "even by the boy that driveth the plough"; it provides the basis for 90 percent of the 1611 King James "Authorized Version" and gave to the English language such expressions as "eat, drink, and be merry," "the fat of the land," "fight the good fight," "the powers that be," and "the signs of the times." Tyndale had to flee into exile to complete his great work but the long arm of the powers that be still had him arrested and strangled in Brussels for heresy. Donne, by contrast, so delighted James I that he became the foremost preacher of his day but is chiefly remembered as an erotic and metaphysical poet whose coinages include "no man is an island," "for whom the bell tolls" and "catch a falling star." **Izaak Walton** (1593–1683), author of *The Compleat Angler* (1653), long worshipped at this unusual octagonal church. Inside there are memorials to **George Calvert, Lord Baltimore** (1580–1632), founder of Maryland, and **Daniel Brown** of Connecticut, the first Anglican clergyman to be ordained expressly for service in America in 1723. In the small churchyard outside there are memorials to **Alfred Harmsworth, Lord Northcliffe** (1865–1922), and **J. L. Garvin**. Northcliffe was Britain's "Citizen Kane," a flamboyant pioneer of tabloid journalism whose *Daily Mail*, still a major daily, became the world's largest-selling newspaper with its first issue. Northcliffe was awarded his viscountcy in 1917 for heading the British war mission in the United

States. Garvin crowned a distinguished journalistic career by becoming editor-in-chief for the 14th edition of the Encyclopaedia Britannica, which, by his time, belied its name and had become an American enterprise, based at the University of Chicago. Above these two stands London's oldest outdoor statue, a contemporary depiction of **Elizabeth I** (permanently regal and youthful, of course!); in the doorway beneath her lurk the battered likenesses of King Lud, legendary founder of London, and his two sons. *Note on the opposite side of Fleet St.* Hoare's Bank, which has stood here since 1690 and numbered among its account-holders both Pepys and, appropriately in view of its name, Nell Gwynne.

Cross Fetter Lane and turn immediately left through a passageway into Crane Court. A modern light above the archway you have come through represents a model of the solar system as it was known in the early eighteenth century (only seven planets, not nine), when the Royal Society met here (1710–80) to discuss learned papers and watch scientific demonstrations. Ben Franklin was elected a member here for his work on electricity.

At the top of Crane Court pass through a crooked passageway on the left, turn right into Fetter Lane and pause by the statue of **John Wilkes** (1727–97). Despite his turbulent political life and stout defense of American liberties and democratic rights (the statue shows him holding a Bill to enlarge the franchise), Wilkes managed to become both a Member of Parliament and Lord Mayor of London. Despite a marked cast in one eye (look at the statue closely!), he was also a notorious womanizer. **Tom Paine** (1737–1809), author of *Common Sense* and *The Rights of Man*, lived in Fetter Lane before taking a leading part in both the American and French revolutions, but his stay in London is unmarked by any memorial.

Retrace your steps and turn down West Harding Street and along Pemberton Row to reach Gough Square and the house where Johnson compiled his celebrated *Dictionary*. A High Churchman and fervent Tory, Johnson

John Wilkes presenting "A Bill for the Just and Equal Representation of the People of England in Parliament." Historian Edward Gibbon thought Wilkes, a notorious womanizer, both well-informed and wonderful company "but a thorough profligate in principle as in practice, his life is stained with every vice, and his conversation full of blasphemy and indecency."

was bitterly opposed to the American Revolution and even wrote pamphlets in defense of government policy, observing with a sneer that "the loudest yelps for liberty" came from "the drivers of negro slaves." This was no mere rhetoric. Johnson's own manservant, Frank Barber, was black and a former slave and eventually became chief beneficiary of the childless author's will. Hence Johnson's much-quoted dictum that "I can love all mankind, except an American." Ironically, the restoration of his home to its original condition involved taking the greatest care of its elegant paneling - American pine.

Pass through Gough Square westwards and under an archway into Gunpowder Square, then right into Wine Office Court and pause outside Ye Olde Cheshire Cheese, a labyrinthine seventeenth-century pub, so rich in literary associations that a sign outside lists such cultural pilgrims as **Mark Twain** and **Theodore Roosevelt** (but misses heavyweight champion **Jack Dempsey**, who may have come for the excellent traditional English fare).

Pass out of the passageway at the bottom of Wine Office Court, turn left, back onto Fleet Street and pause outside the former headquarters building of the *Daily Telegraph*, which has migrated from here to Docklands in East London. The building is now mainly occupied by Goldman Sachs.

Continue east, slightly downhill. On the corner of the next block stands the sadly abandoned former offices of the *Daily Express*, a striking Art Deco exercise in glass and chrome. A cheerfully populist rival to the *Daily Mail*, the *Express* was essentially the creation of the ebullient Ontario-born William Maxwell Aitken, better known as **Lord Beaverbrook** (1879–1964). "The Beaver" was already a millionaire when he arrived in Britain in 1910 and soon became a confidant of **David Lloyd George** (1863–1945), who made him a minister in his War Cabinet. Uniquely, Beaverbrook also served in Churchill's Cabinet during World War Two. A pugnacious champion of the British Empire and an inveterate intriguer, Beaverbrook was also a brilliant publicist, whose leadership enabled the *Express* to oust the *Mail* as the world's biggest-selling daily. H. G. Wells predicted that if "the Beaver" ever got to heaven "he will be chucked out for trying to pull off a merger between Heaven and Hell . . . after having secured a controlling interest in key subsidiary companies in both places, of course."

Note, on the opposite side of the road, Salisbury Court,

The steeple of St. Bride's, Fleet Street, the journalists' church.

where a plaque marks Pepys' probable birthplace. *Next to Salisbury Court stands the headquarters of* Reuter's News Agency, a handsome building of 1935, designed by Lutyens, its entrance surmounted by the trumpet-blowing figure of Fame. Reuter's stands where Wynkyn de Worde established Fleet Street's first printing press in 1500, following the death of his master, William Caxton, the man who first brought printing with moveable type to Britain from Germany.

Pause to look up at the stepped steeple of St. Bride's, the inspiration for the first ever tiered wedding cake, devised by City baker William Rich in the eighteenth century as a special treat to mark his daughter's marriage. When lightning struck eight feet off the spire in 1764 a great debate began. Obviously a lightning conductor was needed. But should it have a blunt end or a sharp one? George III himself was a partisan of the blunt faction, Ben Franklin, inventor of the device, was prominent among the sharp party. No contest. Wags noted that "blunt King George" had to give way to "the sharp-witted American." St. Bride's had already stood on this site for a thousand years when it was destroyed in the Great Fire of 1666. Rebuilt by Wren, it was gutted again in 1940 and restored in 1957. Bride is a corruption of Bridget, an Irish nymphomaniac deity who took "man-eating" quite literally as a method for disposing of discarded lovers.

Cross the road to enter St. Bride's, which has long been "the journalists' church" and has strong American associations. The parents of **Virginia Dare**, the first European child to be born in the American colonies, were married here; there is a small terracotta bust of her at the back of the nave. Virginia's maternal grandfather was John White, the artist who sailed with the Roanoke expedition of 1585 and produced some of the earliest sketches of Amerindian life. The parents of **Edward Winslow** (1595–1655) were married here in 1594 and he himself fell under the spell of St. Bride's fiery Puritan preachers while still an apprentice printer hereabouts. After exile in the Netherlands he sailed with the *Mayflower* and, in an inspired act of lateral thinking, used the iron screw of his printing press to save the ship when it threatened to break up in mid-Atlantic. Winslow served as Governor of New Plymouth three times and was killed leading the expedition ordered by Cromwell to conquer Jamaica. In the middle of the second bay of the screen dividing the north aisle from the nave, at about waist height, can be seen an inscription commemorating two American journalists killed covering the Vietnam War.

Leave the church and turn right, back into Fleet Street. Ludgate House, the last block before Ludgate Circus, on the opposite side of the road, still contains a small branch of Thomas Cook's travel agency. When it was built in 1872–3 it was the firm's London headquarters – hence the exuberant decorations featuring winged cherubs, globes, and carved faces representing the inhabitants of far-flung continents. At its corner, facing onto Ludgate Circus, is a bronze plaque honoring journalist and thriller writer **Edgar Wallace** (1875–1932), who, as a boy, sold newspapers here. Despite churning out 170 books, his spendthrift lifestyle drove him to exile in Hollywood in search of cash to pay off ever-mounting gambling and tax debts. His last project was the script for *King Kong*. Paul Robeson starred as an African chief in the film version of Wallace's 1911 novel of square-jawed British jungle heroics, *Sanders of the River*.

At Ludgate Circus turn right into New Bridge Street and walk south towards the river. At the apex of the archway of No. 14 there is a carved portrait of the boy king **Edward VI** (reigned 1547–53). He inherited the riverside Bridewell Palace, built on this site by Henry VIII as a government guest house. The pious Edward turned it over to the City fathers to serve as a "correctional facility" for wayward women and an orphanage for London's waifs. In the early seventeenth century hundreds of Bridewell children were shipped off to the under-populated American colonies and a chance of premature death far higher than if they had been left to fend for themselves on the foul streets of the capital.

Continue towards the river and Blackfriars station. Walk ends.

En Route: Richard Recommends

Food and Drink

Fleet St. and the side streets off it have numerous sandwich bars, two branches of El Vino's wine bar (Fleet St. and New Bridge St.), and dozens of pubs, including the

Edgar Wallace (Essex St.), Ye Olde Cheshire Cheese (Wine Office Court), the Cock, Tipperary and Punch Tavern (Fleet St.), and the stunningly flamboyant Art Nouveau Black Friar (opposite Blackfriars station). The restaurant of the Wig and Pen Club is open to non-members but prior reservation is advisable. The Wynkyn de Worde in St. Bride's Passage has a varied menu, including vegetarian dishes.

Public Toilets

Eastern end of St. Clement Dane's Church. Junction of St. Bride St. and Farringdon Rd. (turn left at Ludgate Circus).

Delays and Diversions

"The Roman Bath" (Surrey Steps, off Surrey St.) is almost certainly a seventeenth-century fake. The Courtauld Institute Galleries, Somerset House, Strand (£) offer a world-class selection of Old Master and Impressionist paintings including **Manet's** *Bar at the Folies Bergère* and **Van Gogh's** *Self Portrait with Bandaged Ear*, plus others by Botticelli, Breughel, Rubens, Degas, Renoir, Monet, Cézanne, Gauguin, and Toulouse-Lautrec. St. Catherine's House, Aldwych is the HQ of the Office of Population Censuses and Surveys, containing records of births, deaths, and marriages since 1837. A must for family historians. Sir John Soane's Museum, 13 Lincoln's Inn Fields, is the newly-refurbished home of the eccentric architect of the Bank of England, stuffed full of antiquities, casts, prints, and period furnishings. Lincoln's Inn (eastern end of Lincoln's Inn Fields) is another Inn of Court with dignified architecture and delightful gardens; its alumni include St. Thomas More, John Donne, Cromwell, William Penn, and Margaret Thatcher. The Public Record Office (Chancery Lane) has a small exhibition of documentary treasures from the national archives, plus a shop selling invaluable pamphlets and guides for the amateur genealogist and local historian. In Dr. Johnson's House, Gough Square (£), the attic is still set up as it was when he compiled his *Dictionary* there. Portraits, books, and furnishings illustrate the life of the man and his circle.

Shopping and Souvenirs

The BBC shop, Bush House sells tapes and videos of classic BBC radio shows, concerts, Churchill speeches, Shakespeare plays, etc. Much to delight teachers or simply lovers of language, literature, and music as well as radio freaks. Twining's, 2-6 Strand, opposite the Royal Courts of Justice, has hundreds of teas - and coffees - to choose from. Worth popping in just for the smell!

4

The Shadow of St. Paul's: Blackfriars to Monument

This walk penetrates the heart of "the City" proper, the ancient core of London and the center of a hi-tech network of financial operations reaching every corner of the globe. Weekdays this area has a population of over a third of a million, by night and at weekends less than two percent of that number. Choose your preferred time accordingly. Amidst an ocean of humanity fixedly focused on the getting of money, Wren's churches and great Cathedral still survive as islands of serenity.

Starting Point - Blackfriars station (Circle and District lines)

The name of this station is all that remains here of a great Dominican monastery, once so important it was used to store state archives and as a meeting place for Parliament. In 1529, a court met here to consider Henry VIII's proposal to divorce Katherine of Aragon.

Cross the road using the underpass and emerge by the Art Nouveau "Black Friar" pub. *Walk east, under the railway bridge, and turn left to go up* Blackfriars Lane. *To the right you will see* a turning, Playhouse Yard. From 1578 to 1584 and from 1597 to 1642 the former monastery's dining-hall was used as a theater. In this then-fashionable residential area lived playwright **Ben Jonson** and portraitist **Van Dyck**. In 1613, Shakespeare himself bought a house in Ireland Yard, just to the east, off Playhouse Yard, but nothing visible remains.

Continue along Ludgate Broadway until you reach the

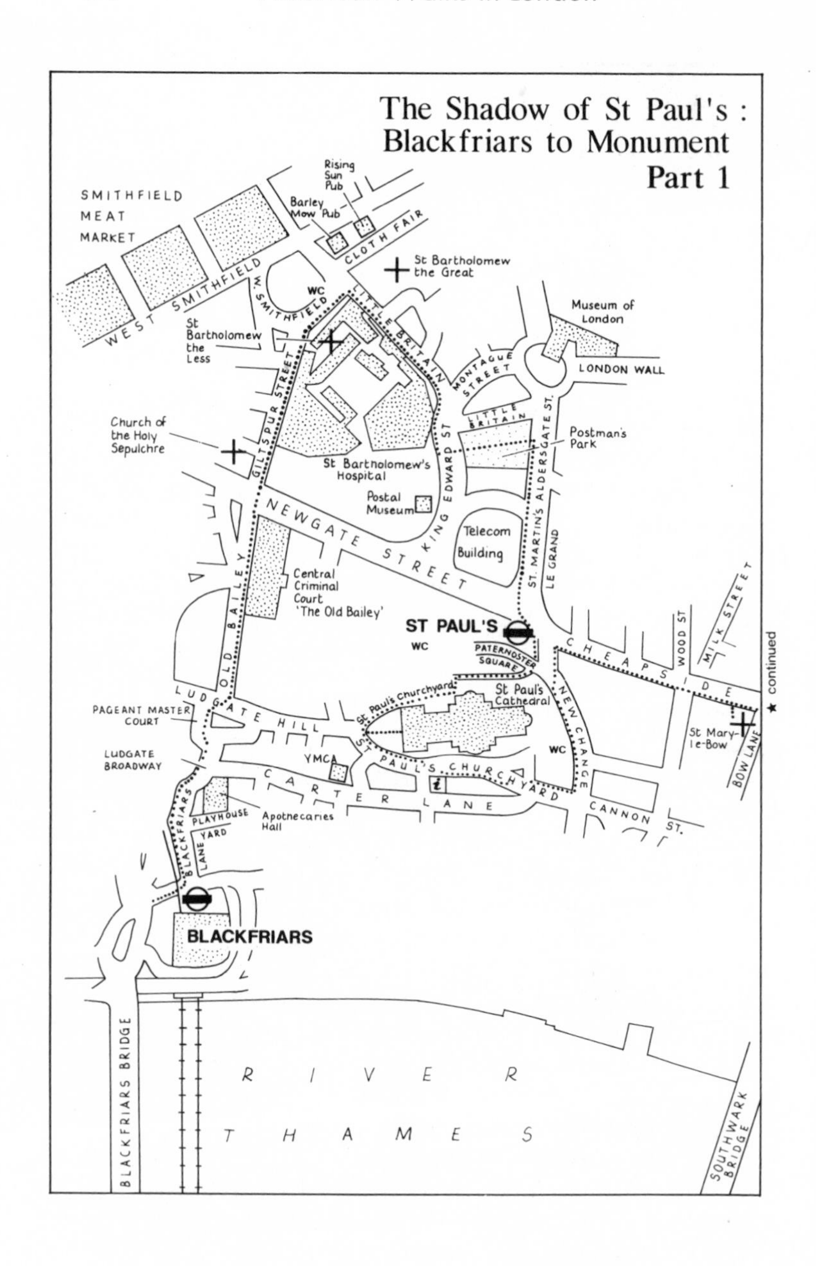
The Shadow of St Paul's :
Blackfriars to Monument
Part 1
SMITHFIELD
MEAT
MARKET
Rising
Sun
Pub
Barley
Mow Pub
CLOTH FAIR
St Bartholomew
the Great
WEST SMITHFIELD
W. SMITHFIELD
WC
LITTLE BRITAIN
Museum of
London
St
Bartholomew
the
Less
MONTAGUE STREET
LONDON WALL
LITTLE BRITAIN
Church of
the Holy
Sepulchre
GILTSPUR STREET
Postman's
Park
St Bartholomew's
Hospital
KING EDWARD ST
ALDERSGATE ST.
Postal
Museum
NEWGATE STREET
Telecom
Building
ST. MARTIN'S LE GRAND
OLD BAILEY
Central
Criminal
Court
'The Old Bailey'
ST PAUL'S
WC
PATERNOSTER SQUARE
CHEAPSIDE
WOOD ST
MILK STREET
continued
LUDGATE HILL
St Paul's Churchyard
St Paul's
Cathedral
NEW CHANGE
PAGEANT MASTER
COURT
St Mary-
le-Bow
BOW LANE
LUDGATE
BROADWAY
YMCA
WC
ST PAUL'S CHURCHYARD
CARTER LANE
CANNON ST.
BLACKFRIARS
PLAYHOUSE YARD
Apothecaries
Hall
LANE
BLACKFRIARS
BLACKFRIARS BRIDGE
RIVER
THAMES
SOUTHWARK
BRIDGE

doorway leading into one of the City's many half-hidden gems, the fine courtyard of Apothecaries' Hall, an oasis of calmness. This institution would certainly have been visited by **Benjamin Silliman** (1779–1864), founder of Yale's schools of science and medicine, of its Trumbull Gallery and of the *American Journal of Science*. It was also known to poet **John Keats** (1795–1821), who qualified as an apothecary in 1816 but immediately abandoned his profession for his Muse.

Follow the winding road through Pageantmaster Court (perhaps a reference to Ben Jonson, who composed court masques for James I?) to reach Ludgate Hill, turn right and pause to note, on the opposite side of the road Ye Olde London, now a pub, but once the London Coffee House and a traditional gathering place for Americans since Ben Franklin's time. In 1799, Bostonian **James Jackson**, future professor of medicine at Harvard, took lodgings here before registering to study at Guy's Hospital. When he returned home the following year he took smallpox vaccine with him to begin America's first vaccination program, in Massachusetts. In 1851, **George Peabody** hosted a celebratory dinner here for 140 guests to mark the success of American exhibitors at the Great Exhibition of Industry of All Nations, held in Hyde Park that year. Ludgate Hill was also the location of another of London's most famous inns, first recorded in 1452 as Savage's Inn and also known as the Bell on the Hoop. After Pocahontas lodged there in 1616–17, the names merged to become the "Belle Sauvage" (beautiful savage). In 1851 publisher **Ernest Cassell** took over the site of the former inn and adopted Pocahontas as his company logo.

Cross Ludgate Hill and turn north into Old Bailey and pause outside the Central Criminal Court. Londoners know this building, rather than the street it stands in, as "the Old Bailey" and associate it with high-profile trials of murderers, traitors, and terrorists. The present (1907) building stands on the site of ancient Newgate prison, which dated back to medieval, perhaps even Roman, times. **William Penn** (1644–1718) was tried here in 1670, for preaching to an unlicensed assembly. In an effort to secure conviction the judge locked up the jurors for two nights without food and then fined them for returning a "Not Guilty" verdict. The jury stubbornly persisted, establishing a landmark in legal history, by asserting their right to independence from overbearing judges. **Oscar Wilde** (1854–1900) was arraigned here in 1895 for sodomy and sentenced to two years hard labor in Reading Gaol. In 1910, London witnessed the trial of Michigan-born **Dr H. H. Crippen** (1862–1910), who poisoned his second wife, cut up her body and buried the pieces in his cellar, then fled to Canada with his secretary and mistress, disguised as a boy. The suspicious captain of the *SS Montrose* contacted British police by radio and Crippen was arrested on landing, the first murderer to be caught by means of the new communications technology. In 1780, the prison was burned down by a gin-crazed mob during the anti-Catholic Gordon riots, an episode vividly described in Dickens's *Barnaby Rudge*. The area in front of the Central Criminal court was where London's last beheading took place in 1820, where in 1864 five pirates were hanged side by side, and where in 1868 the capital's last public hanging took place. The condemned man, **Michael Barrett**, was a member of the Fenians, a secret society of Irish nationalists, based in the United States, which mounted raids into British-ruled Canada and conducted a campaign of terror in Britain itself. In 1867, an unsuccessful attempt was made by Fenians to rescue two comrades held in the Clerkenwell House of Detention (a mile north of here) but an over-generous use of explosive demolished an entire row of nearby houses, killing six of their occupants and injuring fifty more. Barrett was one of those held responsible.

Cross the road and pause outside the Church of the Holy Sepulchre without Newgate, once the largest of more than a hundred parish churches within the single square mile of the City proper. Founded by the courtier-monk Rahere in 1137, it became the traditional point of departure for knights setting out on Crusade – which would take them to the Church of the Holy Sepulchre in Jerusalem. Nowadays the church contains the regimental chapel of one of London's own regiments, the Royal Fusiliers, which is why the churchyard railings are painted in their colors. It is also the burial place of the extraordinary **Captain John Smith** (1580–1631), adventurer, map-maker, and "sometime Governor of Virginia and Admiral of New England," whose life was allegedly saved by Pocahontas. A brass plate on the wall of the south chapel recounts his exploits; he is also depicted in a stained-glass window in the south aisle. The church has a strong musical tradition.

Walk north along Giltspur Street and pause to note the bust of essayist **Charles Lamb** (1775–1834), fixed to the east wall of the church. Lamb was a pupil at Christ's Hospital School, which once stood where the Post Office Yard now is, on the opposite side of the road. He first achieved literary success with the *Tales from Shakespeare* (1807), written for children with his sister, **Mary**.

Continue north and pause to read the inscription underneath the Golden Boy. Tradition has it that this is where the Great Fire of 1666 finally stopped and a former pub once provided a convenient place of business for "resurrectionists," who supplied corpses of the recently-deceased to anatomy students at St. Bartholomew's Hospital across the way.

Follow Giltspur Street round to the right and pause outside the imposing gateway to St. Bartholomew's Hospital, founded here by Rahere in 1123. The statue of **Henry VIII** marks his gracious generosity in hearing the pleas of the City fathers that the hospital be refounded after its royal plundering during the dissolution of the monasteries. In 1568, the Spaniard

Roderigo Lopez was appointed physician here – only to be dismembered at Tyburn in 1594, having been found guilty of attempting to poison Elizabeth I. As one of the few Jews in England at that time he may have provided a model for Shakespeare's Shylock, as the *Merchant of Venice* was written between 1596 and 1598. **William Harvey** (1578–1657), who discovered the circulation of the blood, practiced at "Bart's" for over thirty years. The artist **William Hogarth** (1697–1764), a governor here, painted two murals which can still be seen. The large building on the far, north side of West Smithfield is Smithfield Meat Market, modeled on the Crystal Palace which housed the Great Exhibition of 1851; completed in 1868, it is still the center of London's wholesale meat trade.

Continue to follow Bart's wall along the south side of West Smithfield, passing two memorials. The first commemorates the execution of Scottish patriot **William Wallace** (1270–1305), portrayed by Mel Gibson in the movie *Braveheart*. The second honors the martyrdom of three Protestants, including **John Rogers**, minister of the Church of the Holy Sepulchre just round the corner, the first of some 300 victims of the persecution launched by "Bloody Mary" Tudor (reigned 1553–8) in a vain attempt to return England to Roman Catholicism. *Ahead of you, through an archway under a half-timbered roof, is the entrance* to the twelfth-century church of St. Bartholomew the Great. Much of the church was demolished during the Dissolution and by the eighteenth century parts of what was left had been subdivided for subletting to businesses. **Ben Franklin** worked in a print-shop in part of the former Lady Chapel in the 1720s.

Turn right down Little Britain and follow the road right into King Edward Street, where the Post Office houses the National Postal Museum. The statue outside honors **Sir Rowland Hill**, inventor of the pre-paid, adhesive, uniform-rate postage stamp.

Turn left into Postman's Park and pause to note the unusual covered seating with tile-panels recording acts of heroic self-sacrifice. This was erected at the initiative and expense of fashionable Victorian portraitist **G. F. Watts** (1817-1904), "England's Michelangelo."

Leave the park on the far side and pause to read the plaque on the railings, placed here by the International Methodist Historical Union, which records that hereabouts **John Wesley** (1703-1791) attended a Moravian meeting at which his "heart felt strangely warmed" by the certainty of salvation. This experience was a fundamental turning point in his spiritual development. John and his brother Charles had recently returned from a missionary expedition (1735-38) to the newly-founded penal colony of Georgia; it had been an abject failure, apart from a chance meeting with German Moravian refugees, who had so impressed John that he renewed contact with them on returning to London.

Walk south along St. Martin's-le-Grand and pause outside the modern British Telecom building. This stands on the site of an earlier Post Office building on the roof of which Italian-Irish **Guglielmo Marconi** (1874-1937) gave an epoch-making public demonstration of his invention - wireless telegraphy - in 1896.

Cross Newgate Street, pass the entrance to St. Paul's station and turn right into the pathway called St. Paul's Churchyard (not the churchyard itself) and pause by the plaque, presented by the Pennsylvania Library Association, to honor **John Newbery** (1713-1767) the first publisher to produce books specifically for children. Nearby once stood the home of **Joseph Johnson**, who, in 1791-2, published **Tom Paine's** *The Rights of Man*. Paine discussed his radical ideas here one evening with the poet-engraver **William Blake**, who urged him to flee to France at once - which Paine did. *Behind the railings on the north side of St. Paul's stands* a statue of John Wesley.

Continue westwards and around the front of St. Paul's

This aerial view of St. Paul's, taken in the 1920s, shows how radically the surrounding area has been transformed by war-time bombing and post-war reconstruction.

Cathedral to enter by the door beneath its southwest tower (the one with a clock in it) (£). **Nathaniel Hawthorne** found the Cathedral "unspeakably grand and noble . . . as quiet and serene as if it stood in the middle of Salisbury Plain," but **John Quincy Adams** thought the military memorials all very ordinary and their inscriptions "marvelously insipid." As a scientist **Benjamin Silliman** was much intrigued by the phenomenon of the Whispering Gallery. Features of specifically American interest in St. Paul's include the American Memorial Chapel, four monuments in the south transept (*halfway along on the right-hand side as you face towards the altar*), and a number of memorials in the crypt.

Walk up the (left-hand) north aisle to reach the American Memorial Chapel (behind, i.e., east of, the high altar). This was created as Britain's tribute to the 28,000 American servicemen killed during World War Two while on active service from Britain. Their names are recorded in a Roll of Honor, together with their rank and branch of service. The railings in front of the altar incorporate significant dates in the history of St. Paul's

The High Altar at St. Paul's before its war-time destruction and replacement by the American Memorial Chapel

(its foundation and the completion of its fourth and fifth rebuildings) and of the United States (1607, Jamestown and 1776, the Declaration of Independence). Note the inclusion of tablets representing the Ten Commandments and the Burning Bush, a tribute to Jewish servicemen. The marble floor pattern represents officers' stars of rank. The stained-glass windows bear the arms of the then 48 states. The carved oak and limewood decorations represent American birds and plants.

After leaving the Memorial Chapel pass the marble figure of poet-preacher **John Donne**, wearing his shroud, the only monument of significance to survive the Great Fire of 1666. Donne was actually a shareholder in the Virginia Company and in 1623 preached at the last service held under its auspices.

At the end of the south choir aisle turn left and left again down the steps into the crypt. Turn right and walk to the eastern end of the crypt to find the plain, modest tomb of **Sir Christopher Wren** tucked away beneath an alcove. An engraved slab in the floor nearby marks the last resting-place of **Benjamin West**, alongside his predecessor as President of the Royal Academy, **Sir**

Joshua Reynolds. On a nearby wall is a memorial to illustrator **Randolph Caldecott**; the little girl is holding a replica of the Caldecott Medal awarded annually by the American Library Association for the best American picture book for children. On the far side of the crypt is a memorial to Philadelphian **Edwin Austin Abbey** (1852–1911) who came to England in 1878 and won the praise of Pennell as "the greatest living illustrator." In 1902, he completed a fifteen-panel frieze for Boston Public Library and painted the coronation of Edward VII (reigned 1901–10). Nearby is the dramatic bronze crucifix, a monument to its designer, society portraitist **John Singer Sargent** (1856–1925). Sargent lived most of his life in London and was described as "an American, born in Italy, educated in France, who looks like a German, speaks like an Englishman, and paints like a Spaniard." Duchesses almost literally lined up to be painted by him (at £10,000 a time). His more than 700 canvases include memorable portraits of American novelist Henry James (1843–1916) and Theodore Roosevelt (1858–1919). Many have been surprised at the intense religiosity of the memorial conceived by such a worldly man. The most signal place of honor, *immediately beneath the dome*, is occupied by the majestic sarcophagus (originally intended for Cardinal Wolsey) encasing the remains of **Admiral Horatio Nelson** (1758–1805), killed in the hour of his crucial victory off Cape Trafalgar.

On a wall just beyond Nelson's tomb and three steps up to the left is a memorial to Pilot Officer **William Meade Lindley Fiske III**, "an American who died that England might live." A Cambridge graduate, Billy Fiske captained the U.S. four-man bobsled team to victory and gold at the 1928 Winter Olympics when he was just 16 and did it again in 1932. Stockbroker, filmmaker, and socialite, he married a Countess of Warwick, joined 666 (the Millionaire's) Squadron in the front line of the Battle of Britain, shot down a German plane on his first mission and crash-landed after his second amid a raid on his home base, Tangmere in Sussex. Snatched from the wreckage by devoted air-crew, he died of his injuries the next day. His grave, which is still tended, is marked with the inscription "He was one of us." Note his pilot's wings beneath the inscription.

Three steps up to the right from Nelson's tomb is a bust of **George Washington**, presented by President Harding in 1921. Note nearby the new monument to the dead of the Gulf War.

On leaving the crypt (by the stairs you used to enter it) pause at the top of the steps to note above its entrance a monument to **General Robert Ross** (1766–1814), whose men looted and burned Present Madison's Washington residence in retaliation for the burning of York (Toronto). The scorch marks were painted over, thus making it thereafter "The White House." Ross was killed in battle shortly afterwards at North Point, Maryland.

Next to the south transept doorway stands a memorial to Majors-General **Pakenham** and **Gibbs**,"who fell gloriously" attacking New Orleans on January 8, 1815 – after peace had been signed between Britain and the U.S. but still in time to afford Andrew Jackson a famous victory and set him on the path to the Presidency. Nearby, *opposite Flaxman's memorial to Nelson* (note how the sculptor deals with the Admiral's missing right arm and eye), stands a huge monument to **General Cornwallis** (1738–1805) which tactfully omits any mention of his role as commander of the British forces whose surrender at Yorktown in 1781 effectively marked the end of the Revolutionary War.

Before leaving the Cathedral pause to note the imposing pulpit where, on December 6, 1964, **Dr. Martin Luther King, Jr.** preached on "The Three Dimensions of a Complete Life" before journeying on to Oslo to receive the Nobel Peace Prize.

Outside the Cathedral pause at the rear of the statue of **Queen Anne** (reigned 1702–14), a grossly flattering

An image problem for the colonies? America represented at the foot of Queen Anne's statue.

representation of a monarch who stood five feet tall and weighed 300 pounds. The female figures grouped around the plinth stand for the realms to which she laid claim - Britain, Ireland, France, and America (complete with feather headdress and a severed head underfoot).

Turn left along the south side of the Cathedral, passing statues to the martyr **St. Thomas à Becket** (reclining in the shrubbery) and, on the opposite side of the road, to 1,025 firefighters of the wartime Blitz, *and then turn left up New Change and right into* Cheapside. This was London's main shopping street until retailing shifted its center of gravity westwards in the last century. The names of side turnings (Wood St., Milk St., Bread St.) reveal their origins in medieval commerce.

Churchill called them "the heroes with dirty faces." Over a thousand London firefighters died during the Blitz.

Cheapside to Monument

Continue east to reach Bow Churchyard, beside the church of St. Mary-le-Bow, *and pause* to admire the swaggering statue of **Captain John Smith**, every bit as tough and arrogant as his pose suggests. A mercenary at 16, he once slew three Turks successively in single combat, was enslaved and imprisoned (in a harem) from which he escaped to England – via Russia! Almost all his tall tales, once dismissed as empty bragging, are now believed to be true. The statue, unveiled in 1960, is a replica of one in Richmond, Virginia. Tradition holds that the only true cockneys are those born within range of the sound of "Bow bells."

Continue along Cheapside and turn left (north) up King

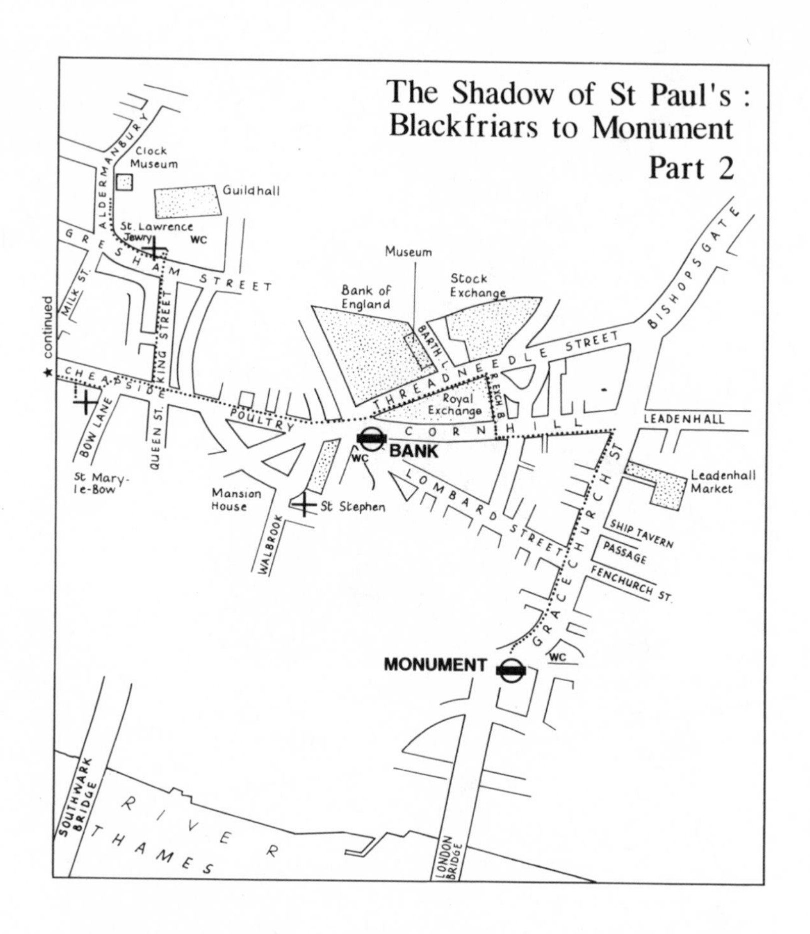

Street to reach Guildhall Yard. Fifteenth-century Guildhall is the ceremonial seat of government of the Corporation of the City of London and the setting for banquets hosted by the Lord Mayor in honor of state visitors. Between 1768 and 1774, on the very eve of the American Revolution, the Member of Parliament for the City was actually an American, Barlow Trecothick of Massachusetts. In 1775, when **John Wilkes** (see p. 45) was Lord Mayor, numerous letters from outraged American activists, including John Hancock, were read

The braggart who told the truth – Captain John Smith

out here to assembled City merchants, who strongly sympathized with their grievances. The beautiful Wren church of St. Lawrence Jewry (rebuilt 1671–7) contains commemorative windows to both **Wren** and to **St. Thomas More** (1478–1535) whose *Utopia* may have been inspired by the discovery of the "New World" in 1492. A side-chapel also has stained-glass windows featuring the arms of Commonwealth countries, including Canada.

Walk west under the modern concrete archway out of Guildhall Yard and turn right into Aldermanbury to see a bronze bust of **Shakespeare** – a memorial to two of his fellow-actors, **Condell** and **Hemming**. After his death, they collected his plays for posterity and made possible the printing of the First Folio in 1623. *Just* *beyond this* a small garden is all that remains of St. Mary Aldermanbury, dismantled and re-erected at Westminster College, Fulton, Missouri as a monument to Churchill in 1966, the year after his death and twenty years after he delivered his famous "Iron Curtain" speech there, calling for a continuation of the wartime Anglo-American alliance in the face of Communist expansionism.

Retrace your steps via Guildhall Yard and King St. to return to Cheapside and turn left to reach Bank junction. *To your left* looms the Bank of England and beyond that rears the Stock Exchange, standing where ex-bareknuckle prize-fighter Mendoza the Jew ran a boxing academy around 1800. **Daniel Mendoza** was all-comers champion of England in 1791 and defended his title twice successfully - despite being 5 feet 7 inches tall and weighing in at only 160 pounds. He wrote the first scientific treatise on *The Art of Boxing* and is credited with inventing rapid combination punching rather than relying on mauling and slugging it out, the standard tactic of his heavier opponents. *Ahead* is the porticoed Royal Exchange, in front of which stand statues of the **Duke of Wellington** and **J. H. Greathead**, the engineer whose improved tunneling shield made possible the construction in 1891 of the Northern Line which runs under your feet, through what was for decades the world's longest tunnel (17 miles). *Beyond* Greathead's statue you can see Lloyd's Bank, where **T. S. Eliot** was grateful to escape school-teaching by accepting secure, if dull, employment before finding his true metier in publishing. References to commuters' zombie-like progress from London Bridge to this area occur in *The Waste Land*. *To the right* is the Mansion House, official residence of the Lord Mayor of London, where **Nathaniel Hawthorne** much enjoyed the lavish hospitality - until his Mayoral host bluffed him into making a speech.

Use the underpass to cross to the left-hand (north) side

The man who invented the charitable foundation – George Peabody

of the Royal Exchange, walk along and turn right behind it to pause by the statue of **George Peabody**. The statue was cast by American sculptor **William Wetmore Story**, who worked in Rome, where Peabody, went for the sittings. The trip proved no tonic for Peabody, who died shortly after the statue was unveiled by the Prince of Wales. Peabody's offices were just across the way from here in Old Broad Street. His business was taken over by Junius P. Morgan.

*Walk past a memorial to **Julius Reuter**, founder of the worldwide news agency and turn left into Cornhill. On the opposite, south side of the road*, the door of No. 32 is carved with scenes from the history of this ancient street, including the famous meeting at which novelists Charlotte and Anne Brontë revealed their true, female identities to an astonished Thackeray and their publisher. *Somewhere along here* once lived **Squanto** (died 1622), London's earliest recorded American resident. Captured by English freebooters in 1605, he lived in England until 1614, when Captain John Smith returned him to his native New England - only to be taken away again and sold into slavery in Spain, from which he escaped back to England *again* and was returned once more to America in 1619. In 1621, Squanto came into contact with the Pilgrim settlers of Plymouth Plantation and served as interpreter to Edward Winslow, during negotiations with his adoptive people, the Wampanoags, Pocahontas' tribe.

At the eastern end of Cornhill turn right into Gracechurch Street, where Penn was arrested for unlicensed preaching in 1670 *and follow it south, crossing the road into Fish Street Hill, to reach Monument station (Circle/District lines). Walk ends.*

En Route: Richard Recommends

Food and Drink

The YMCA (Carter Lane, off Ludgate Broadway) offers good value in an overlooked location. The crypt of St. Paul's Cathedral (no entry charge) has excellent coffee. The Museum of London café is stylish and always has vegetarian offerings, as does the atmospheric cafe in St. Mary-le-Bow Church. Ye Olde London (Ludgate Hill) offers lunchtime pub grub in its downstairs bar and an unexpected garden. Other pubs en route include The Magpie and Stump (Old Bailey), the Viaduct Tavern (Newgate St.), the Barley Mow and Rising Sun (Cloth Fair, just off West Smithfield), the Half Moon (Leadenhall Market), and the Swan Tavern (Ship Tavern Passage). Three hostelries off the south side of Cornhill retain strong historical associations: Simpson's Tavern in Ball Court, the George and Vulture in Castle Court, and the Jamaica Wine House in St. Michael's Alley, where a plaque marks the site of London's first coffee-house.

Public Toilets

Crypt of St. Paul's Cathedral, West Smithfield, Paternoster Square (north of St. Paul's), by St Paul's Choir School (New Change), in Aldermanbury, and at Bank station.

Delays and Diversions

The Central Criminal Court, Old Bailey is open to the public but cameras are strictly forbidden within the precincts.

St. Bartholomew the Great, West Smithfield, London's oldest church, has a cavernously impressive interior and the tombs of **Rahere** and **Sir Walter Mildmay**, founder of Emmanuel College, Cambridge, alma mater of **John Harvard** and numerous New England Puritan divines.

The National Postal Museum, King Edward Street has a world-class collection of British and Commonwealth stamps.

St. Botolph, Aldersgate has vivid stained-glass windows showing James I in procession and Wesley preaching. Search out (west wall at the rear of the nave) the monument of 21-year-old Catherine Mary Meade of Philadelphia, with its touching verse epitaph.

Museum of London, London Wall (£; multiple re-entries on same ticket; free after 4:30; closed Mondays). The history of London from prehistoric times to the Blitz. Also the home of the Lord Mayor's coach, a star exhibit.

The Guildhall Clock Museum, Aldermanbury, also has a display of historic playing cards.

St. Stephen Walbrook (behind Mansion House). Wren's miniature masterpiece, a silent explosion of pure light, containing *The Martyrdom of St. Stephen* by **Benjamin West**.

Bank of England Museum, Bartholomew Lane. A revelation too often passed by.

St. Vedast, Foster Lane has a stunning ceiling – severe yet splendid.

Leadenhall Market, off Gracechurch Street. Exotic Victorian engineering which still contrives to be a real market, with fresh game and produce.

Shopping and Souvenirs

St. Paul's Cathedral Crypt has outstanding quality souvenirs, representing English lifestyles. The City Information Centre (south side of St. Paul's Cathedral) for City of London publications and souvenirs (cufflinks, ties, tie-clips, etc.). Museum of London shop sells books and quality souvenirs relating to London; especially good for children's gifts. The National Postal Museum has pamphlets, postcards, models, and souvenirs for the keen philatelist. Guildhall Bookshop sells books, maps, and posters on London, City of London souvenirs, and historic playing cards. Bank of England Museum has surprisingly off-beat souvenirs, often incorporating monetary motifs, from paperweights to suspenders for trousers, plus coins, money-boxes, the famous "Bank Black" ink for calligraphers, and videos and books relating to Kenneth Grahame, a Bank employee and the author of the children's classic book, *The Wind in the Willows*.

5

Tower, Thames, and Travelers: Monument to Borough

This walk covers the eastern part of the City, skirting the historic Pool of London, between London Bridge and Tower Bridge, which was, until the 1960s, still part of the working port. The same conditions obtain as with Walk 3 - on a weekday there will be crowds and noise, especially around lunchtime; at weekends or in the evening you will have the place to yourself, but there will be fewer places open for food and drink - except around the Tower of London, roughly the half-way mark. Also most of the churches will be locked. There are a lot of potential diversions along this route, and much of interest for literary buffs, but opportunities for shopping are limited.

Starting Point - Monument station (Circle and District lines)
Leave the station by the exit leading onto Fish Street Hill and pause to look downhill to your right. Fish Street Hill is an ancient Roman street. Londoners have been walking up and down it for almost two thousand years. Originally it led straight onto London Bridge. The present bridge is some yards upstream, to your right as you look downhill. At the bottom of the hill is Sir Christopher Wren's church of St. Magnus Martyr, a Viking pirate and Earl of Orkney - a reminder of London's historic links with Scandinavia. In *The Waste Land,* T. S. Eliot describes the interior as "inexplicable splendour of Ionian white and gold." It was gutted by

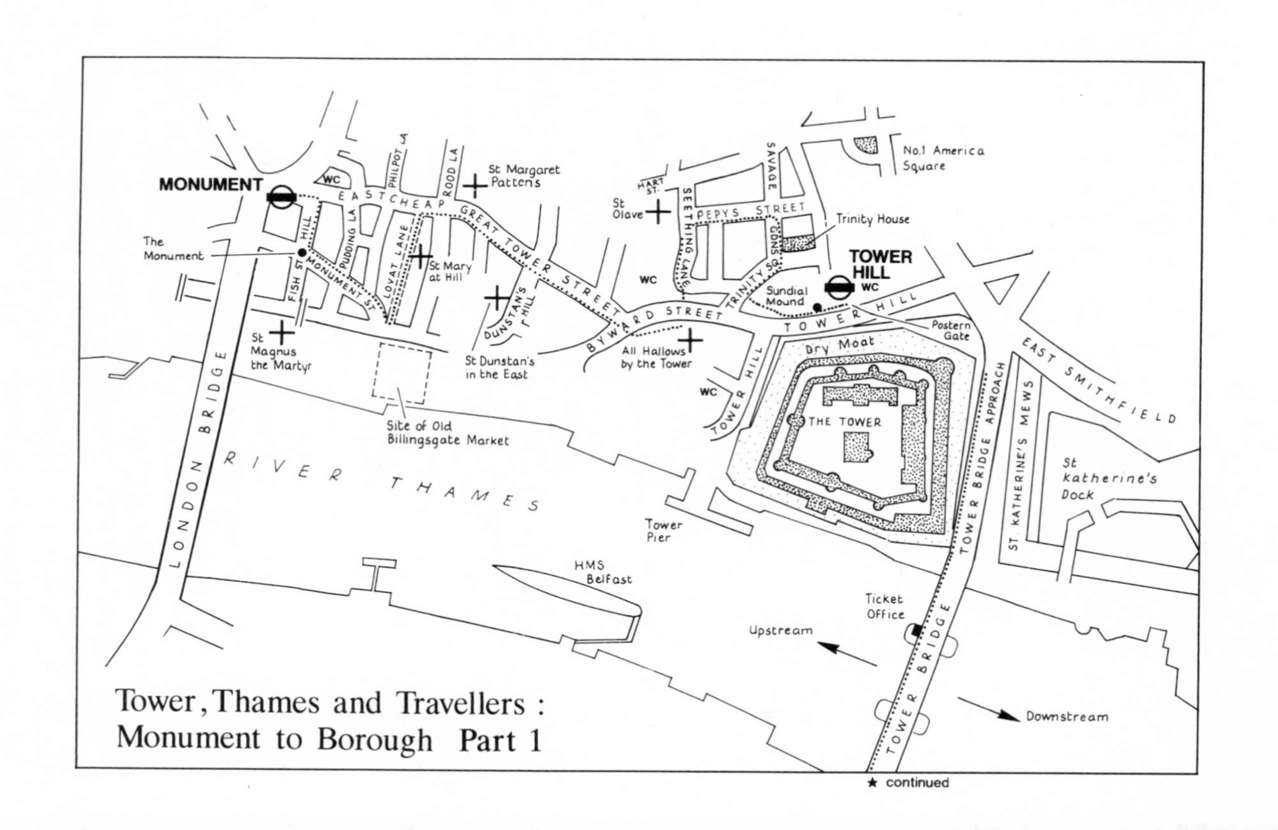

Tower, Thames and Travellers : Monument to Borough Part 1

The Monument to the Great Fire of 1666. Charles II, hand on hip, supervises the reconstruction of London.

fire in 1995. A pitted but sturdy chunk of a Roman wharf can be seen in the porch beneath the spire. In medieval times this riverside area between London Bridge and the Tower was the most crowded part of the City, with some twenty parishes and their respective churches crammed into a few score acres.

Walk downhill a few yards to where you can see the low-relief carving on the western face of the Monument, designed by **Wren** and City Surveyor **Robert Hooke**, to commemorate the Great Fire of London of 1666, symbolized by the golden fireburst on top. Originally Wren suggested a statue of Charles II but the monarch objected on the grounds that *he* hadn't started the fire. Instead he is depicted in **Cibber's** wonderful carving, supervising the reconstruction of the stricken city in a languidly arrogant pose, reminiscent of his cousin, Louis XIV of France. Behind him stands **James, Duke of York**, the future James II. On the north face of the Monument the story of the fire is carved in Latin (English translation underneath!). Notice the missing line at the bottom of the inscription, which blamed "Popish frenzy" for the fire and were removed after the full restoration of civil liberties to Roman Catholics in 1829. The inscription on the south face describes the recovery of the City after the disaster.

Walk down Monument St. to the corner of Pudding Lane. A plaque records where the Fire started on September 2, at the home of Thomas Faryner, royal baker. At the end of a long, hot summer the City was tinder dry and, fanned by a strong east wind, the flames soon spread to the riverside wharves, packed with combustible timber, rope, tar, canvas, etc. With the river cut off, there was no hope of fighting the fire and the flames were soon over three hundred feet high (half as high again as the Monument). Londoners simply fled. Under the energetic direction of the Duke of York, gangs of sailors used gunpowder to blow up houses and create firebreaks, but basically the fire burned itself out over the course of four days, devouring St. Paul's, 80 churches, and 13,000 houses, but claiming only eight lives.

Continue downhill and glance to the right to note Sir Horace Jones' Billingsgate fish market (1877), surmounted by Britannia.

Turn left up Lovat Lane, a narrow twisting, cobbled passage, medieval in atmosphere on a quiet day, which leads northwards onto Eastcheap, the site of a meat market in the Middle Ages. Shakespeare's Falstaff is supposed to have been a "regular" at the Boar's Head which once stood at the western end of this street. *Across the road you can see* a range of Victorian office buildings. The one on the corner of Philpot Lane, to the left, has a frieze of dogs' heads at the top. Nos. 33–35 (1868), dead ahead, are described by Professor Pevsner as "one of the maddest displays in London of gabled Gothic brick." Look for the boar's head in the central arch. What can that have signified?

Continue right (east) along Eastcheap and pause opposite the church of St. Margaret Pattens, which takes its name from the wooden soles once made hereabouts and worn to protect soft shoes from mud and sharp rocks. Rebuilt by **Wren** in 1684–7, the church has some of the last canopied pews to be seen in London; one, with "CW" carved on its roof, may well have been Wren's pew.

Continue into Great Tower St. and Byward St., cross the busy road at the bottom with care and pause at All Hallows by the Tower, which has stood here since Saxon times - at least four centuries longer than the Tower of London itself. Diarist **Samuel Pepys** watched the Great Fire from the tower of this church. A blue cartouche at the corner records that **William Penn** was baptized here. **John Quincy Adams**, sixth President of the United States, married here.

Cross back over Byward St. to the north side via the underpass, turn right as you come out, then right into Seething Lane and turn into the railed gardens (locked at weekends) to see a striking modern bust of **Samuel Pepys**, who worked in the Navy Office which once stood here. At the end of the street stands St. Olave's, Hart St., a survivor of the Great Fire. Pepys and his feisty wife are both buried there; her beautiful monument was placed to look down on his pew. The macabre gate with its spiked skulls inspired Dickens to dub it "St. Ghastly Grim" in *The Uncommercial Traveller*. The church has a strong link with Norway, is named after its warrior-saint-king Olaf, and always has a Norwegian flag hanging inside.

Turn right down Pepys St. and pause at the corner of

Savage Gardens to look up at the impressive bulk of No. 1, America Square, an immense office building sited where New England timber merchants congregated in the eighteenth century.

Turn right down Savage Gardens to enter Trinity Square. *On your right*, at No. 10, is the imposing former headquarters of the Port of London Authority (1922) and *on your left*, with cannons placed outside it, is Trinity House (1792–4), which has been supervising the training of pilots and maintenance of lighthouses since the reign of Henry VIII. *As you move away from it you will be able to see* its sailing ship weather vane. This whole area is a reminder of the great importance of shipping and the sea in the history of London. *Walk round the railed garden and enter it by* the gate at its western edge. *To your left, marked off by chains, you will see* the execution site known as Tower Hill, where more than a hundred historic personalities forfeited their lives, most notably **Saint Thomas More**. Test your knowledge of British history and see how many more you can recognize. The first couple were victims of the Peasants' Revolt. Others date from the shaky beginnings of the Tudor dynasty (after 1485), the ill-tempered reign of Henry VIII, and the see-saw politics of the Civil War and Restoration period (1640s–1660s).

Go down into the gardens, a memorial to the sailors and fishermen who died at sea in World War Two. The 132 bronze panels contain the names of lost ships and their crews. North American names like *Cadillac, California, Canadian Star, Empire Bison, Puerto Rican*, and *Quebec City* are a poignant reminder of how many were sunk in the Battle of the Atlantic. From the number of names it looks as though the whole crew of the *Ceramic* perished. In many other cases only the Master appears to have done so. A seaman in the merchant marine was four times more likely to be killed than a sailor in the Royal Navy. Most ships were naturally registered in

The Tower from the river. The buildings on the left have changed radically.

British ports but others were from Norway, Greece, Belgium, and Hong Kong.

Leave the sunken garden by the left hand (eastern) steps. The temple-like structure you see is a memorial to the seamen of World War One, designed by **Sir Edwin Lutyens**, architect of the Cenotaph, which is covered with the names of sunken ships and their crews.

Leave the railed garden and climb up the mound surmounted by a large sundial. Around its base significant dates in the history of London are cast in bronze. The Peasants' Revolt is wrongly dated as 1387 (actually 1381). The seats here offer the opportunity to rest, look across to Her Majesty's Palace and Fortress, the Tower of London, and ponder its long and momentous history. **Sir Walter Raleigh** was imprisoned here for 13 years, consoled by the comforts of tobacco. The Bloody Tower, refurnished to look as it did when he was living there, now contains reproductions of the first European pictures of Native American life, painted by **John White** in 1585. **Henry Laurens**, former president of the Continental Congress, was imprisoned in the Tower for over a year in 1780–81, having been taken on the high seas en route for Holland to negotiate

When this photograph of the Tower's Yeoman Warders was taken it was still customary for them to be recruited only from servicemen decorated for gallantry.

a commercial treaty and a loan of $10,000,000 to support the rebel colonists' fight for independence. Closely confined, Laurens became ill, emaciated, and deeply embittered. On a lighter note, **Nathaniel Hawthorne**, like any other tourist, brought his family here in 1855 to see the Crown Jewels and thought the Yeoman Warders (Beefeaters) "looked very much like the kings on a pack of cards, or regular trumps." In 1917 an advance guard of the American Expeditionary Force marched into the Tower, to the applause of the British garrison, the only occasion in history when foreign troops have entered it as free men, rather than as prisoners. Their commander, young **Captain George Patton**, stayed up all night drinking with his hosts before departing for the front at 4:30 a.m.

Leave the sundial mound and turn right down the steps, past the ticket-hall of Tower Hill station. *On your left you can see* a section of the original wall which once ran right round Roman Londinium. Note the lacing-courses of reddish tile, inserted at three-feet intervals to keep the structure steady. The statue of **Trajan** is an eighteenth-century reproduction. Trajan conquered part of what is now Romania but has no known connection with London. *Set in the wall to his right you can see* a reproduction of the tombstone of **Classicianus**, the wise financial director who revived Londinium's commercial prosperity after it had been sacked during the revolt of Queen Boudicca in AD 60–61. Fragments of the tomb were found around here during the middle of the last century when the sewers and underground railway were being constructed. The original tomb can be seen in the British Museum.

Trajan hails passengers emerging from Tower Hill station. To his rear stands the original Roman wall of Londinium and, set into the modern wall, a facsimile of the tomb of Classicianus.

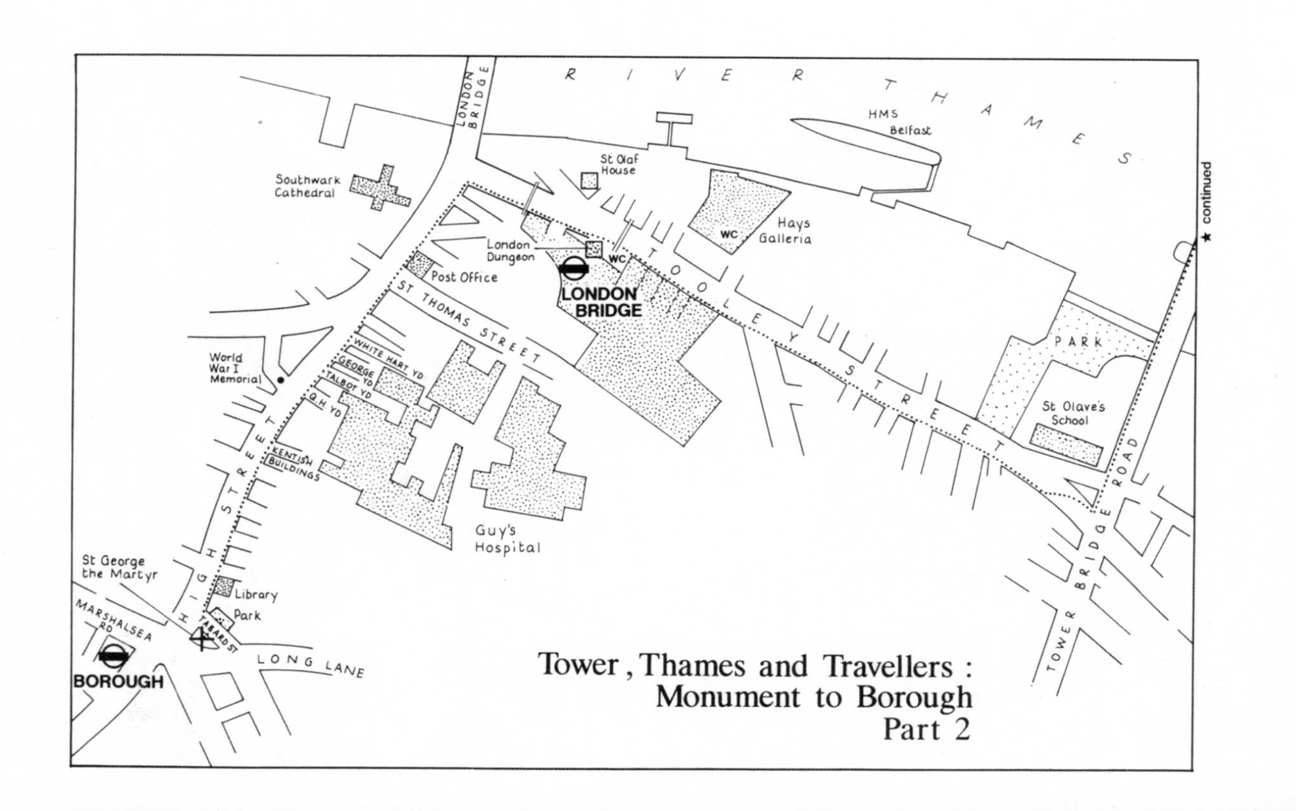

Tower, Thames and Travellers : Monument to Borough Part 2

The Pool of London as seen from the tower of St. Magnus Martyr in the 1950s, when it was still very much a working part of the river. The transformation since then has been dramatic.

Cross under the road using the underpass and turn left at the ruins of the Postern Gate (not up the steps) and along the pathway looking down on the dry moat of the Tower, which was drained in 1843 on the order of the Duke of Wellington, then Constable of the Tower. He thought it was a health hazard and, as many of the Tower's toilets emptied straight into it, he was probably quite right. The moat was used as a place of execution as recently as 1941, when a German spy was shot there by firing squad.

Turn right up the stairs and walk towards Tower Bridge. As you look across the road, through the gap between the buildings you can see St. Katherine's Dock, now a yacht marina, but originally a secure storage area for valuable cargoes. *Beyond the masts note* the Ivory House, a fine example of early industrial architecture (1854), incorporating sturdy iron pillars and now converted to shops and apartments. *Just before you go onto Tower Bridge look down to the right* onto the Tower waterfront. Here in 1887 **"Buffalo Bill" Cody**, accompanied by **Annie Oakley**, unloaded his Wild West Show from the steamship *State of Nebraska* (named for his home state), before the wondering eyes of a crowd of cockneys. Tower Bridge itself was built in 1894, the latest thing in hi-tech steel engineering, but given a pseudo-Gothic stone cladding to make it look less strikingly modern next to the venerable Tower of London.

Tower Bridge Road to Borough

Stop by the Tower Bridge ticket office and look at the metal panel which explains the marvelous panorama unfolded before you upstream. On a fine day this is a great spot for a photograph. In mid-stream you can see *HMS Belfast*, now a branch of the Imperial War Museum, permanently anchored here. At 10,500 tons she was the largest cruiser ever built for the Royal Navy, took part in the bombardment of the Normandy beaches on D-Day – and could in theory hit Hampton Court Palace, fourteen miles up-river.

As you reach the far side of Tower Bridge pause to look back and downstream. Unless it's a very misty day you should be able to see Canada Tower, a soaring, shining, silvery structure with a pyramid top. Designed by **César Pelli**, this 800-foot skyscraper stands at the heart of London's regenerated Docklands and is Britain's tallest building. Built in 1991 by the Jewish Reichmann brothers, its name honors their adopted country.

Turn right into Tooley Street, past the former St. Olave's school. The bust with its back to you is of **Ernest Bevin**, dockers' union leader, Foreign Secretary, and architect of NATO. The statue honors energetic **Samuel Bevington**, Bermondsey's first mayor.

Continue along Tooley Street. The park to your right gives a fine view of the Tower on the far side of the Thames. Until the 1960s, this side of the river was crowded with working wharves and warehouses. Since then it has been redeveloped to house offices, smart

St. Ghastly Grim – St. Olave's, Hart St., the parish church of Samuel Pepys

restaurants, and visitor attractions such as the London Dungeon. St. Olave's school and Art Deco St. Olaf House at the far end of the street commemorate **Olaf of Norway** (he of the Hart Street church), who came to the aid of London in 1014 and used his fleet to pull and burn down London Bridge from under the very feet of a besieging Danish army. A Norse saga recorded triumphantly that "London Bridge is fallen down, Gold is won, and bright renown!" Six centuries later these words resurfaced in a child's nursery rhyme.

At the end of Tooley Street turn left past London Bridge Station, the capital's oldest terminus, dating from 1836, and into Borough High St. You are now in Southwark (pronounced "Sutherk"). This part, known simply as "the Borough," was for centuries the center of the hop trade. Hops, used to give English beer its distinctive bitter taste, were grown in Kent, to the southeast of London, and could conveniently be brought here, where breweries were crowded together along the southern side of the Thames - from which they took their water. As the sewers also emptied into the Thames, beer brewed hereabouts no doubt had a very distinctive flavor. As wheeled vehicles were banned on old London Bridge, Borough High Street was where all stagecoaches from the south had to stop. Consequently it was lined with coaching inns, offering accommodation to travelers. As you pass along this street note numerous narrow turnings which once led into inn yards. In some cases the shape of the yard is preserved, even though surrounded by modern offices. Many are still cobbled and one or two have stone mounting blocks to help riders get on their horses. The best example is a turning called Kentish Buildings, on the left, almost at the end of the street.

Continue down the left-hand side of the street. Pause by the Post Office where a plaque informs you that on this site the first Bible in English was printed in 1537.

Cross St. Thomas Street but pause to glance down it towards Guy's Hospital, where poet **John Keats** once studied. *Walk on until you come to the second turning on the left* called White Hart Yard. Here a plaque reminds you that the White Hart Inn appears in the writings of both Shakespeare, as the HQ of rebel Jack Cade in *Henry VI*, and of Dickens, where Mr. Pickwick first meets Sam Weller, whose knowledge of London was "extensive and peculiar." *Next, pause outside No. 67 to look up* at the flamboyant fascia of W. H. & H. Le May, Hop Factors. *Pause again and glance to the left* at No. 77 to see into the yard of The George, London's last galleried inn, dating from 1677 and an absolute gem. *Walk on and look to the right to see* a striking memorial to the local dead of World War One. Unusually, one of the carved panels on the plinth depicts an airplane in combat. Beyond it is a black, gate-like doorway which was once part of a local prison. *The next turning on the left* is Talbot Yard, its name a corrupted reminder that here, from 1306 to 1875, stood the Tabard Inn, from which Chaucer's immortal pilgrims departed for Canterbury. And not even a plaque to mark the spot! *The next turning after that* is Queen's Head Yard. Low down on the building just before it a plaque does mark the former site of the Queen's Head, the pub owned by John Harvard's mother, the sale of which enabled him to endow Harvard College. *On the opposite side of the road from the local library*, named in honor of John Harvard, a plaque marks the site of the majestic home of gigantic **Charles Brandon**, Duke of Suffolk, Henry VIII's brother-in-law and jousting partner.

Just before you reach the church at the crossroads turn left into Tabard St. and left again into a small park. The wall running along its northern edge is all that remains of the Marshalsea Prison. Dramatist **Ben Jonson** was incarcerated here for unwisely lampooning Scots in a play, a couple of years after Scottish James Stuart had ascended the throne of England. Charles Dickens' father was imprisoned in the Marshalsea for debt until a legacy fortunately released him. **Dickens** made him the model for Mr. Micawber, ever confident that good fortune was just around the next corner.

Cross to the church of St. George the Martyr (1736), which plays a significant part in Dickens's *Little Dorritt*. The heroine is both christened and married here. The ill-fated American poet **Sylvia Plath** married English poet **Ted Hughes** here in 1956. Returning to the U.S., she taught at Smith College and he at the University of Massachusetts. In 1960, they came back to England. Sylvia's first volume of poetry was published to acclaim, prompting a $100 contract from the *New Yorker*. In 1962, Hughes left her and she took her own life the following year. Ted Hughes, renowned for his savage nature poems, is now the Poet Laureate.

Walk ends. Borough station is just across the road (Northern line).

En Route: Richard Recommends

Food and Drink

Following the route will take you past Indian, Italian, Chinese, and even a Peruvian restaurant, plus a Macdonald's and a traditional fish-and-chip shop. The dense concentration of office workers around Borough High St. means it is packed with sandwich bars and fast food outlets. The George (77 Borough High St.) is one of the nicest pubs in London for setting, service, and atmosphere.

Public Toilets

Gracechurch St. (junction with Fish Street Hill), at the Tower of London, Tower Hill station, and in Hay's Galleria, off Tooley Street.

Delays and Diversions

The Monument can be climbed - 311 steps! Apart from the churches mentioned it is worth visiting St. Mary at Hill (entrance in Lovat Lane) (Wren 1670–6) and St. Dunstan-in-the-East (turn south off Great Tower St., down St. Dunstan's Hill), now a ruined shell but a very lovely one, an ideal setting for a sandwich lunch. To visit the Tower of London allow at least two hours and preferably four; the Crown Jewels are a must. At the Postern Gate (underpass to Tower Hill station) is a tile panel marking the start of the Wall Walk; follow the succeeding twenty-odd panels and you'll traverse the eastern and northern sections of the Roman Wall of Londinium and end at the Museum of London. Boats go up and down river from Tower Pier. St. Katherine's Dock has moored Thames sailing barges and a lightship, plus shops and restaurants. Tower Bridge, modestly advertising itself as "The Most Famous Bridge in the World," tells the story of its own construction; the walkway between the two towers at the top gives stunning views along the river, which should appeal to keen photographers. The Design Museum covers the application of design in everyday life in the twentieth century. Nearby is a Tea & Coffee Museum. "Churchill's Britain at War" relies on special effects to evoke an era. *HMS Belfast*, just opposite, is the real thing. The London Dungeon just before London Bridge station is for those who like their history bloody.

Shopping and Souvenirs

All Hallows by the Tower has facilities for making your own brass-rubbings. The numerous shops around the Tower sell the usual run of souvenirs. The Tower itself has four souvenir shops, including a large one outside the Middle Tower entrance. Hay's Galleria (Tooley St.) has elegant shops and stalls as well.

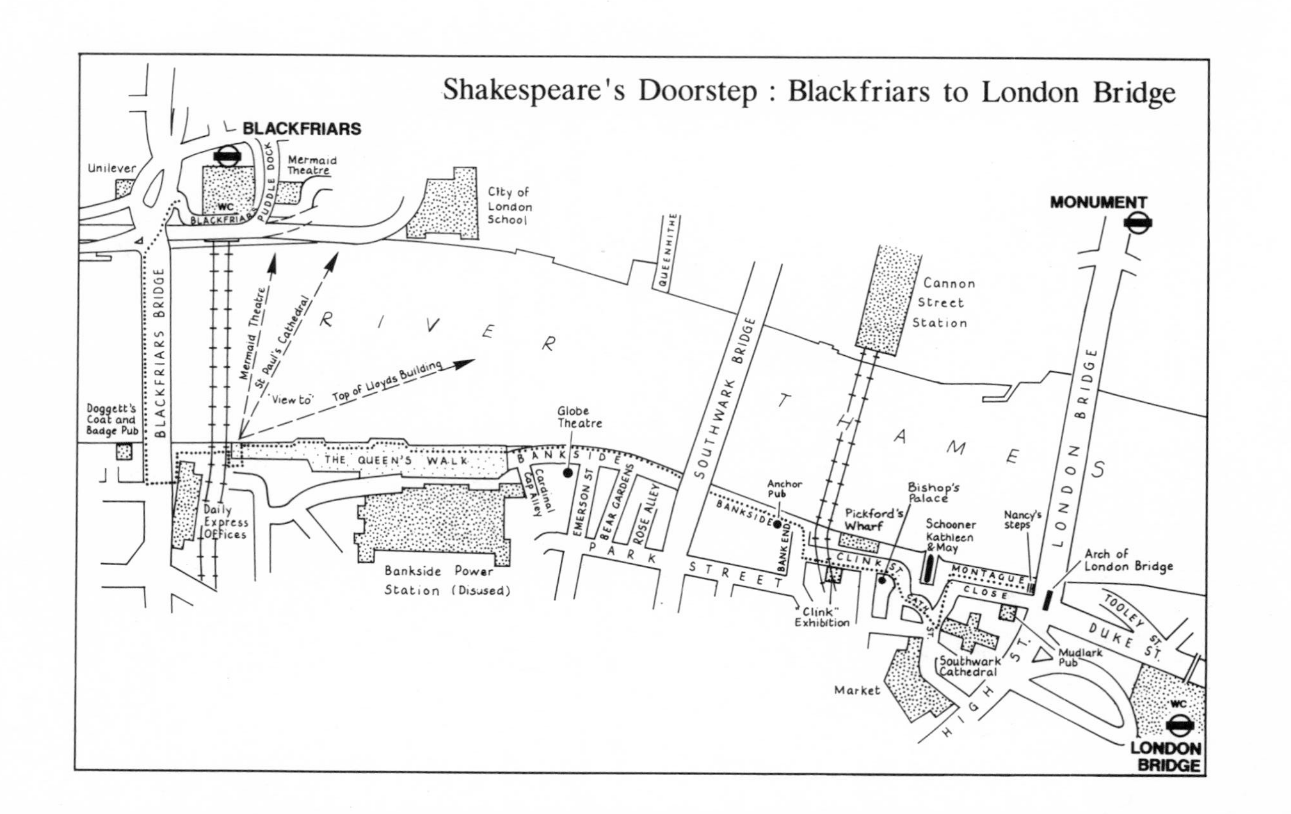
Shakespeare's Doorstep : Blackfriars to London Bridge
BLACKFRIARS
Unilever
WC
BLACKFRIARS
PUDDLE DOCK
Mermaid Theatre
City of London School
MONUMENT
QUEENHITHE
Cannon Street Station
RIVER THAMES
BLACKFRIARS BRIDGE
Mermaid Theatre
St Paul's Cathedral
'View to'
Top of Lloyds Building
Doggett's Coat and Badge Pub
Globe Theatre
SOUTHWARK BRIDGE
LONDON BRIDGE
THE QUEEN'S WALK
BANKSIDE
Cardinal Cap Alley
EMERSON ST
BEAR GARDENS
ROSE ALLEY
PARK STREET
Daily Express Offices
Bankside Power Station (Disused)
Anchor Pub
BANKSIDE
BANK END
Bishop's Palace
Pickford's Wharf
CLINK ST.
"Clink" Exhibition
Schooner Kathleen & May
Nancy's steps
MONTAGUE CLOSE
Arch of London Bridge
TOOLEY ST.
DUKE ST.
Mudlark Pub
Southwark Cathedral
Market
HIGH ST.
WC
LONDON BRIDGE

6

Shakespeare's Doorstep: Blackfriars to London Bridge

This short walk, through a neglected area now rapidly reviving, takes in two major attractions with strong American connections – the reconstructed Globe Theatre and London's *other* Protestant Cathedral, Southwark. Opportunities for shopping are limited.

Starting Point – Blackfriars station (Circle and District lines)

Leave the station by exit no. 3, pass a statue of Queen Victoria and cross onto Blackfriars Bridge. (It was originally to be named in honor of Pitt the Elder, but Londoners would have none of that.) The handsome 1930s Art Deco building on the opposite side of the road is the headquarters of Unilever, an Anglo-Dutch corporation specializing in products such as soap powders and margarine. Notice the statues near the roof-line, including Dutch girls in national costume and Japanese ladies in kimonos. The site was formerly occupied by the gigantic De Keyser's hotel, established by a Belgian waiter who rose to become London's first Catholic Lord Mayor. The next building to it, looking upriver, was formerly the City of London Boys' School, adorned with statues of **Shakespeare** and **Francis Bacon** (held by some to be the real author of Shakespeare's plays). The neo-Gothic building next to that, Sion College, houses a major theological library.

As you cross the bridge notice the bays attached to its piers (more clearly seen from down on the opposite

Blackfriars Bridge *c.*1910. De Keyser's Hotel (left) was replaced by the Unilever headquarters in 1930–1. To the right a chimney and factory building show industry very much in evidence along the riverside at this time.

bank); shaped like pulpits, they are a reminder that the Blackfriars (Dominicans) were a preaching order. The huge columns in the river are remnants of the first (1862–4), unsatisfactory railway bridge which crossed here. The splendid badge of the London, Chatham and Dover Railway company at the southern end bears a white horse, symbol of Kent, and the county motto "Invicta" (Unconquered) plus the coats of arms of London, Chatham, and Dover. *At the end of the bridge glance across* at a modern pub – Doggett's Coat and Badge – "themed" around rowing. **Thomas Doggett**, comedian, manager of the Theatre Royal, Drury Lane and a patriot fiercely loyal to the new Hanoverian dynasty established in 1714, celebrated that event by inaugurating an annual rowing race, from here upstream to Cadogan Pier, Chelsea, the prize being a splendid orange-red coat with a silver badge representing Liberty. A winning waterman could always be sure of good custom while wearing this unmistakable uniform. Although taxis long ago ousted watermen in

An artist's impression of the riverside *c.*1900. Note the distinctive Thames sailing barges in the right foreground.

the passenger trade the race is still held and is the oldest annually contested event in the British sporting calendar.

Turn left down the steps, past the new offices of the *Daily Express*, originally founded by Canadian tycoon Max Beaverbrook (see p. 47) *and at the bottom turn left into the underpass to see* the fine illustrations of the road and railway bridges at different dates. *Next look across the river* to see the new (1980s) brick buildings of the City of London School.

Continue along the riverside walkway under a massive brick arch, pass the Founders' Arms pub and pause to take in the view across the river, showing (left to right) the Mermaid Theatre, St. Paul's Cathedral, and the top of Sir Richard Rogers' controversial Lloyd's Building. *Go on past* the former Bankside Power Station. Designed by **Sir Giles Gilbert Scott**, like his other monster creation, Battersea Power Station (built 1948–63), this was located right by the river, so that coal could be brought to it by water, rather than in trucks which would add to London's traffic congestion. Like Battersea, it became redundant by 1980 but, rather than falling into decay, was scheduled in 1995 to be converted into an extension of the Tate Gallery, housing its collection of contemporary art.

Continue along the riverside walkway until you come to a small group of houses at Cardinal Cap Alley in the shadow of the reconstructed Globe Theatre. It is claimed that **Katherine of Aragon** landed here when she first came from Spain to England to marry the future Henry VIII's elder brother, Arthur. He died shortly after their wedding, leaving her to be passed on to Henry. After twenty years of marriage to her, but no male heir, Henry tried to ditch her by claiming that their marriage had been contrary to the prohibited degrees of kinship as set out in Leviticus and should therefore be annulled. As he had persuaded the Pope to set aside this objection in the first place, this wouldn't wash. It is also claimed that **Sir Christopher Wren** used the narrow house here as his office while building St. Paul's, so that he could, as it were, stand back and see the immense project in perspective. (Bear in mind that the view would not have been blocked by riverside offices as it is now.) The house certainly dates back to the sixteenth century and was at one time an inn. The Globe Theatre, reconstructed on its original site, is a reminder that Bankside, being outside the walls of the City proper and beyond the jurisdiction of its magistrates, was for centuries London's red light district, where visiting sailors and citizens alike could get drunk, visit a playhouse or a whorehouse, and watch animals being tormented to death (hence Bear Gardens). The Globe has been reconstructed using, as far as possible, the materials and methods of Shakespeare's day, with massive oak timbers being held together by wooden pegs, not nails. It is the first thatched roof building to be constructed in London since the Great Fire of 1666. Open to the sky, this "Wooden O" makes possible the re-enactment of plays as they were presented in Shakespeare's day, in mid-afternoon, without artificial lighting, but, thanks to the enclosed space and apron stage, far better acoustic control than was possible when plays were put on from trestles in courtyards, as the strolling players in *Hamlet* did. Although many illustrious theatrical names have lent their support to the Globe project, its realization was essentially due to the vision and energy of Chicago-born actor-director **Sam Wanamaker** (1919–93), who founded a trust to accomplish the project in 1970 and died just before its completion, but was honored with the rank of CBE (Commander of the British Empire) and an honorary Doctorate from the University of London.

On the opposite side of the river you can see an indentation in the straight line of the bank – Queenhithe, the main unloading point for ships from Saxon times till the fifteenth century.

Continue along the riverside walkway, where there is a helpful map of the area, and pass under Southwark Bridge to reach the Anchor pub (1775), from which there is a good view across the river to Cannon Street station (1866). The station roof was destroyed by wartime bombing and a modern office complex was inserted over the platforms in the 1980s as the electrification of the line had done away with the need for space for smoke and fumes to disperse. The Communist Party of Great Britain was founded in Cannon Street Station Hotel in 1920. Originally the sprawling riverside palace of the Roman governor of Londinium occupied this site.

Bear right and then left and pause just before Cannon Street Railway Bridge and note a plaque at head height, which records the misfortunes of three precursors of the Pilgrim Fathers, martyred for their faith in 1593. *Next on your right* is the Clink, a gruesome visitor attraction. Its name, an English slang synonym for prison, recalls the private lockup of the Bishop of Win-

Cannon Street station before the insertion of its modern office complex above the platforms.

chester, whose palace precinct once stood here and whose word was law. The Bishop did not, however, scruple to benefit from the profits of brothels hereabouts, which masqueraded as bath-houses and were staffed by the "Winchester geese," so called for their elegant necks.

Next on your right, at Pickford's Wharf, you will see the excavated remains of the fourteenth-century dining-hall of the Palace. *Look up to note* the miraculously surviving rose window, whose stained glass would have been stunningly illuminated each evening by the rays of the dying sun.

Continue past the schooner *Kathleen and May,* whose moorage is a reminder that locals once had the privilege of unloading cargo at the staithe (landing-place) here, free of the usual tolls.

Bear right into Cathedral St. a few yards until you see a Victorian covered vegetable market to your right *and turn left and left again to enter* Southwark Cathedral. This mainly thirteenth-century building, much restored, occupies a site on which a Roman villa stood. For most of its history it was a priory and then a parish church, and was only elevated to cathedral status in 1905.

Immediately to your left as you enter there is a panel of blind arcading in the Early English style, which is one of the oldest fragments of the original building (*c.* 1220). *Pass the striking font and look left to see* a display of grotesquely carved bosses taken from the medieval wooden roof. *Above the windows along the north aisle* are portraits of famous persons associated with the Cathedral, such as **Dr. Johnson**, (whose friends, the Thrales, owned a brewery nearby), Johnson's friend **Oliver Goldsmith, John Bunyan**, and **Geoffrey Chaucer**. Next there is a doorway, part of which dates from Norman times, then the tomb of Chaucer's friend, the poet **Gower** (1325–1408), his head resting on three books, written respectively in Latin, French, and English. *In the north transept is* the elaborate tomb of a local pharmacist, whose hilarious epitaph promotes his patent pills from beyond the grave. *Continue eastwards and go left down steps to enter* the striking Harvard chapel, a tribute to **John Harvard** (1607–38), who was baptized here when it was the parish church. The window (presented by Ambassador Joseph H. Choate in 1905) bears the arms of Harvard College and of Emmanuel College, Cambridge, Harvard's own alma mater. There is also a wall-plaque memorial to composer **Oscar Hammerstein II**. *After leaving the chapel and continuing eastwards, pause to note* the rare wooden figure of a thirteenth-century Crusader knight in mail armor. *Pass through the chapel dedicated to AIDS victims and adjacent chapels to enter* the south aisle, where the statuette of a Romano-Celtic hunter-god stands opposite the tomb of the vastly learned **Lancelot Andrewes** (1555–1626), chairman of the working party which produced the Authorised Version, "King James Bible" of 1607. *Continue to the point where the aisle joins the south transept and read on the right-hand column* a heart-wrenching seventeenth-century epitaph to a ten-year-old girl. *The south transept, to your left*, contains a monument to **William Emerson** (died 1575), a supposed ancestor of Ralph Waldo Emerson. *After crossing the transept note* another memorial to the distinguished Bohemian engraver **Wenceslaus Hollar** (1607–77), who created wonderful panoramic views of London, using an imaginary platform several hundred feet above this cathedral as his vantage point. Pause by the impressive monument to **Shakespeare**, whose younger brother Edmund is buried here. If you look carefully at the carved panorama behind the reclining Shakespeare you should be able to pick out the Globe, the Bishop of Winchester's Palace, and the traitors' heads on spikes above the gatehouse of old London Bridge. The windows above show characters from the plays, comedy to the left, tragedy to the right.

Leave the cathedral where you entered, turn right and right again to reach a cobbled area between the cathedral and the river. *Go forward past* the Mudlark pub, whose name and sign recall the homeless children of Dickens's day who scavenged along the foreshore for lost or waste items to sell or recycle. *Ahead stands* the sole surviving arch of the second London Bridge. The first stone London bridge (1209), one of the wonders of Europe, with 150 houses and shops on it, was finally demolished in 1830; but its successor was so sturdy that it began to sink into the river under its own weight. It was this structure that was disassembled and re-erected at Lake Havasu City, Arizona. The present London Bridge dates from 1972. *To the left you will see* a flight of steps, with a kink halfway up them. The second London Bridge was brand-new when Dickens wrote *Oliver Twist* and set a crucial scene at this very spot. Here the luckless Nancy betrays the whereabouts of the kidnapped Oliver, but is overheard by Noah Claypole, concealed by the kink in the steps (try it!) – thus sealing her fate at the hands of a vengeful Bill Sykes.

Go up "Nancy's Steps" to find yourself by a dragon marking the southern boundary of the City of London.

Walk ends. London Bridge station (Northern line) is just

across the road or cross the bridge to reach Monument (District and Circle lines).

En Route: Richard Recommends

Food and Drink

There are over a dozen sandwich bars and restaurants (Italian, Indian, Japanese, Thai) around London Bridge station and a café/restaurant in the Chapter House of Southwark Cathedral. The pubs mentioned above all serve pub grub.

Public Toilets

Foot of the stairs leading down from Blackfriars Bridge to the riverside, and at London Bridge station.

Delays and Diversions

The Globe (£) tells the story of Bankside in Shakespeare's day and the theater's rebirth.

The Clink Prison Museum (£) offers a sex-and-violence interpretation of the locality's history.

Old Operating Theatre and Herb Garret, St. Thomas's St. (£). Medical time-warp in a church roof and tower.

Shopping and Souvenirs

Southwark Cathedral has books, stationery, and CDs.

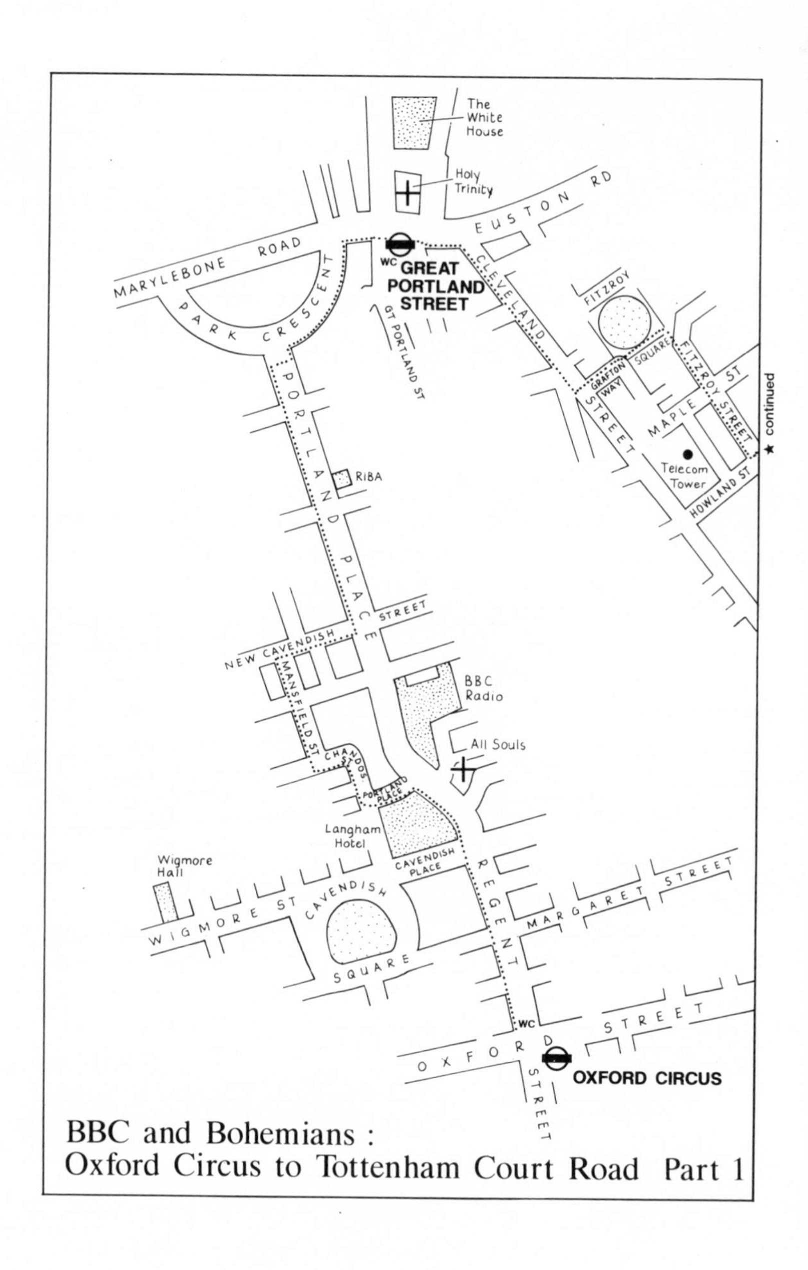

BBC and Bohemians :
Oxford Circus to Tottenham Court Road Part 1

7

BBC and Bohemians: Oxford Circus to Tottenham Court Road

Our route passes through Marylebone and "Fitzrovia." Marylebone, an upmarket residential area around 1800, now accommodates embassies and the discreet offices of professional associations. "Fitzrovia" was *meant* to be upmarket but soon became a sort of down-at-heel "Latin Quarter," much favored by artists and writers. The houses of Fitzrovia quickly became subdivided into tiny workshops for subcontractors in the furniture and musical instrument trades. Nowadays the dominant presence is of students, medical personnel, and employees of the advertising/PR/video businesses. Between them they support a good range of varied and good value eating places.

Starting Point - Oxford Circus Station (Central, Bakerloo, and Victoria lines)

Walk north along the west side of Upper Regent Street and pause outside No. 309, now part of the University of Westminster but in 1909 Regent St. Polytechnic, where American poet **Ezra Pound** (1885–1972) lectured part-time.

Continue northwards to the church of All Souls, Langham Place, with its unusual needle-pointed spire and corona, built (1822–24) by **John Nash** (1752–1835), whose bust stares out from the steps leading up to the entrance. Nash, the favorite architect of the Prince Regent, later George IV (reigned 1820–30), obliged his patron by marrying one of his discarded mistresses.

Ouch! – The eccentric needle-point spire and corona on All Souls, Langham Place, the BBC church and long-time home of radio's " The Daily Service."

Regent St. and Regent's Park, both Nash creations, are named for the Prince. The BBC's long-running "Daily Service" is broadcast from here on Radio 4. *Immediately north of All Souls is* Broadcasting House, purpose-built in 1932 as the headquarters of the BBC and now the main home of BBC Radio. The statuary above the main entrance, by **Eric Gill** (1882–1940), represents Prospero, the magician, and Ariel, his "ayrie spirit," from Shakespeare's *The Tempest*. Notice the "radio wave" motifs on the entrance doors and running round the building at first-floor level. (Were the designers unsure whether radio waves were zig-zagged or curved?) At the height of the Blitz **Ed Murrow** broadcast live to America from the rooftop, describing the chaos around him, his calm but vivid commentary punctuated by the crackle of anti-aircraft fire, the crash of high-explosive bombs, and the rumble of falling masonry. He so impressed the BBC that he was offered the post of Deputy Director-General, which he declined. The British government was so impressed that they offered him an honorary knighthood, which he accepted. Colonel **Glenn Miller's** experience of the BBC was far less happy. After his first broadcast some listeners wrote to complain that they could only pick up his band's louder passages, so BBC officials demanded that he play at a constant volume. Miller tried in vain to explain that it was contrasts in volume that helped to make the "Glenn Miller Sound" distinctive. Neither side would give way, so the BBC canceled all his planned future broadcasts, despite an avalanche of furious protests from frustrated fans.

Bear left and pause in front of the Langham, one of London's earliest luxury hotels, dating from 1864. Its famous guests have included the American writers H. W. Longfellow, Mark Twain, and Bret Harte. Its nearness to the Wigmore Hall gave it a distinguished musical clientele, including the Czech composer **Antomin Dvořák** (1841–1904), who, as Director of the New York Conservatory (1891–5), dubbed his most popular, ninth symphony *From the New World*, and **Arturo Toscanini** (1867–1957), conductor of New York's Metropolitan Opera House and of the New York Philharmonic and creator of the National Broadcasting Orchestra of America. A wartime direct hit on the Langham's water-tanks did its decor no good at all and condemned it to dowdy decades as an overflow office block for the BBC, until it was acquired by the Hilton chain and lavishly refurbished.

Continue forwards and then right into Chandos Street. **Washington Irving** took rooms at No. 3 in 1829 when he became secretary to the American Legation in London. It was a double homecoming because his merchant father had been born British (but sided with the rebel cause during the Revolution) and because Irving had already visited England in connection with the failing family business and made useful literary connections with Sir Walter Scott and his publisher John Murray. Encouraged by them, he published his *Sketch Book* (1819–20), which includes an essay about Westminster Abbey and brought him accolades on both sides of the Atlantic. As the first native American writer to make a reputation outside his own country, Irving was awarded an honorary Oxford degree. After his diplomatic appointment ended in 1831, he stayed on in London to finish the *Tales of the Alhambra*, based on his sojourn in Spain in 1826–9. When he returned to the States in 1832 after an absence of seventeen years he was feted at a huge celebratory dinner and promised his rejoicing fellow-countrymen that he would *never* go abroad again. He duly returned to London in 1842 and again in 1846.

At the top of Chandos Street bear left and turn immediately right into Mansfield Street. In 1861 historian and diplomat **Charles Francis Adams** (1807–86) moved into No. 5, then the American Embassy, now Orbis House. The outbreak of the U.S. Civil War made this a peculiarly sensitive moment in Anglo-American relations and Adams was acutely anxious to avoid any unnecessary antagonisms. Unfortunately, a difficulty immediately arose over what he should wear when presenting his credentials to Queen Victoria. His predecessors, at the express direction of the American Secretary of State, had eschewed formal court dress, with its silk stockings and gold lace, in favor of plain black suits. This gesture of republican simplicity was interpreted in high circles as disrespectful to the monarch and an ostentatious, if inverted, display of moral superiority. Adams dithered until a helpful British acquaintance

The last façade. Adam decor is still visible above the entrance to the former home of American banker Joshua Bates at 46 Portland Place.

discreetly murmured that among the English upper classes a plain black suit was the conventional uniform of a butler. Adams opted for the glitz. No. 13 bears a blue plaque showing it to be the former home of architect **John Loughborough Pearson** (see p. 35) and then of architect **Sir Edwin Lutyens** (see p. 48). At No. 20 opposite lived **Charles, third Earl Stanhope** (1753-1816), an outspoken opponent of British efforts to crush American independence. Despite being the brother-in-law of the younger Pitt, he also advocated peace with revolutionary France as well. A versatile man of science, he invented a calculating machine, printing processes, and a type of microscopic lens which bears his name.

At the end of Mansfield Street turn right into New Cavendish St. and pause to note the plaque at No. 61 to **Alfred Waterhouse** (1830-1905), architect of the monumental Natural History Museum at South Kensington. Waterhouse, who came of stern Quaker stock, actually wanted to be an artist, but his family considered this a frivolous ambition, so he opted for architecture instead.

Turn left into Portland Place, London's second widest street, laid out between 1774 and 1778 by the Adam brothers. Nos. 46–48, designed by James Adam, are the only surviving originals whose delicate facades give some idea of what the street must once have looked like. No. 46 was the home of American millionaire banker **Joshua Bates**, who generously founded the Boston Public Library but still opted to become a naturalized British subject. No. 54 was the home of historian **James Bryce** (1838–1922) who wrote a classic account of U.S. politics, *The American Commonwealth* (1888), and served with distinction as British Ambassador to Washington between 1907 and 1913, but regarded the Panama Canal (opened in 1913) less as a triumph of American engineering than as "the greatest liberty that man has taken with Nature."

Continue north to pass, on the opposite side of the road, the Royal Institute of British Architects. In 1939, **Frank Lloyd Wright** (1869–1959) lectured here on "The Architecture of Democracy." The statues along the middle of Portland Place commemorate **Quintin Hogg**, founder of the nearby Regent Street Polytechnic, **Sir George White**, a Field-Marshal who also won the Victoria Cross (the British equivalent of the Congressional Medal of Honor), **Lord Lister**, pioneer of antiseptic surgery (hence "Listerine" mouthwash), and the **Duke of Kent**, fourth son of George III, whose sole significant achievement was to father Queen Victoria. At No. 63 a blue plaque marks the former residence of **Frances Hodgson Burnett** (1849–1924), who was born in Manchester, England but moved to Knoxville, Tenn. in 1865. Her children's classic *Little Lord Fauntleroy* (1886) tells the story of an American boy who inherits an English earldom. The immense popularity of this book condemned generations of small boys, dressed in "Fauntleroy" velvet suits and lace collars, to squirm in agonies of embarrassment before studio photographers while posing for formal portraits. (The get-up was in fact inspired by Oscar Wilde's flamboyant "Aesthetic" garb, which Gilbert and Sullivan had already lampooned in *Patience* (1881).) A quarter of a century later Mrs. Burnett repeated her success with another children's classic, *The Secret Garden* (1911). No. 76 was the home of **Lord Tweedsmuir** (1875–1940), who, under the pen-name **John Buchan**, wrote his bestselling espionage thriller *The Thirty-Nine Steps* (1915) while living here. (And had his hero, Scottish mining-engineer Richard Hannay, take rooms here on returning from South Africa.) British-born director **Alfred Hitchcock** made a stunning film version, starring Robert Donat, in 1935, and there were further but inferior re-makes in 1959 and 1978. Despite a busy career as lawyer, academic, war-time propagandist, and MP, Buchan made the time to write over fifty books and crowned his career by serving as Governor-General of Canada from 1935 until his death.

Continue to the northern end of Portland Place and cross the road to where a blue plaque records where the U.S. Embassy stood from 1863 to 1866 and Pulitzer Prize-winning historian **Henry Brooks Adams** (1838–1918) continued to serve as secretary to his ambassador father, **Charles Francis Adams**, after their move from Mansfield Street. Their main task, to keep Britain from recognizing the Confederacy, became increasingly easier after the Union victory at Vicksburg and Lincoln's proclamation ending slavery. Hundreds of Britons passed through this building during those few years, on their way to fight as volunteers in the ranks of the Union army.

Follow the road to the right round Park Crescent (1819–1821), one of Nash's most elegant creations. *Continue right onto* what is now the Marylebone Road/Euston Road. This was opened in 1756 as the "New Road," London's first "by-pass," built so that cattle-drovers from the Thames Valley to the west of the capital should no longer have to clog up the traffic along Oxford Street on their way to the markets and abbatoirs at Smithfield. Underneath this stretch of road runs the

A vision realized – Nash's Park Crescent.

oldest section of London's Underground, opened in 1863 as the world's first sub-surface railway.

Pause to note a bust of President **John F. Kennedy**, a replica of the one in the Library of Congress by American sculptor **Jacques Lipchitz**, paid for by British subscribers to a fund organized by the *Sunday Telegraph*. The 50,000 donations were limited to a maximum of £1 each. The bust was unveiled in May 1965 by Kennedy's brother, Robert. The President's official memorial is a plot of land at historic Runnymede, where Magna Carta was negotiated between King John and the barons in 1215, ceded in perpetuity to the United States.

On the opposite (north) side of the road note the church of the Holy Trinity by **Sir John Soane** (1824–28) and

The Ambassador's son.

featuring an unusual external pulpit. Its fashionable congregation once included the Duke of Wellington, painter J. M. W. Turner, Prime Minister W. E. Gladstone, and nursing pioneer Florence Nightingale. Like so many London churches, it is now redundant and has found a new role as the headquarters of the Society for the Promotion of Christian Knowledge. *Beyond it you can see* the "White House," built in 1936 as luxury "service apartments" but now an hotel.

Cross the road to pass Great Portland St. station and turn right down Cleveland St. where **Samuel Morse** (1791–1872) and **Charles Robert Leslie** (1794–1859) lodged at No. 141, when they were both studying painting under Benjamin West. Morse, better known as the inventor of Morse code, was a talented portraitist and also founded America's National Academy of Design. Leslie, born in London of American parents, excelled in paintings of everyday scenes and went on to write biographies of Constable and Reynolds. The two young artists led an energetic social life, and writers **Charles Lamb** and **Samuel Coleridge** were both frequent visitors to this address. Morse found the din of traffic in this street *very* trying.

Continue along Cleveland St. to turn left at Grafton Way and enter Fitzroy Square. The east and south side, built in severe gray Portland stone, were the last great building project of **Robert Adam** in the 1790s. The stuccoed north and west terraces came a generation later (1827-1832). Maverick Cambridge economist **John Maynard Keynes** (1883-1946) once shared No. 21 with avant-garde painter **Duncan Grant** (1885-1978). Keynes's views on the possibilities of a planned economy had a profound influence on F. D. Roosevelt's "New Deal" recovery program and on postwar American governments' commitment to the maintenance of full employment. He also played a prominent part in the 1944 conference held at Bretton Woods, New Hampshire, which set up the International Monetary Fund. Keynes's last major service to his nation was to negotiate a multi-billion dollar loan from the U.S. to Britain in 1945. Heaped with honors, having made a vast personal fortune, married a Russian ballerina and written a book that revolutionized economics, Keynes at the end of his life expressed only one regret - that he had not drunk more champagne. No. 29 was from 1887 to 1898 the home of **George Bernard Shaw**. During this period he wrote *Mrs. Warren's Profession*, *Arms and the Man*, *Candida*, and *The Devil's Disciple*. A strident socialist, once described as "a Puritan who missed the Mayflower by five minutes," Shaw was nevertheless very fussy about what he ate and wore. He left this address to marry a wealthy woman who could well afford to keep him in the austerity he claimed to pro-

Artistic address: plaques marking the former home of G. B. Shaw (and mother) and Virginia Woolf (and brother and dog) at 29 Fitzroy Sq.

fess. Married or not, Shaw continued to fascinate women, though that is usually as far as it went. Libertine Frank Harris observed scornfully that Shaw was "the first man to have cut a swathe through the theatre and left it strewn with virgins." In 1907, No. 29 became the home of **Virginia Woolf** (1882–1941). She was already building her reputation as a critic in the pages of the *Times Literary Supplement* but had yet to start her first novel. No. 7 was the home of **Sir Charles Eastlake** (1793–1865), first Director of the National Gallery. At the Royal Academy Summer Exhibition of 1860 he directed the Duchess of Sutherland to inspect *At the Piano*, submitted by the youthful **J. A. M. Whistler**, who had but recently established himself in nearby

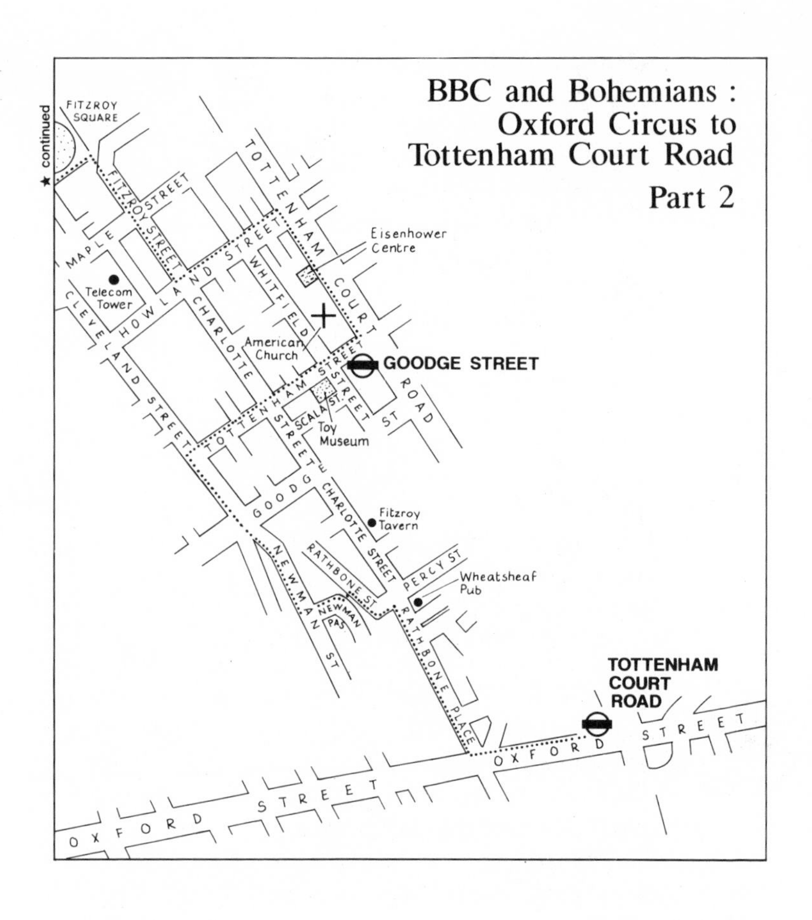

Newman Street. Eastlake praised it as "the finest piece of painting in the Royal Academy." It sold for thirty guineas. Whistler was on the way up – where, of course, he had always assumed he belonged anyway.

Fitzroy Street to Tottenham Court Road

Turn south into Fitzroy St. The statue of the Venezuelan revolutionary **José de Miranda** (1750–1816) is a reminder of London's nineteenth-century role as a refuge for political exiles and of Britain's active encouragement of the break-up of the Spanish empire in Latin America. In 1895, **Whistler** had a studio at the back of No. 8, which was later taken over by his former assistant, the Anglo-German **Walter Sickert** (1860–1942), who later gave Churchill painting lessons – though not here!

Continue south, turn left into Howland St. and cross Whitfield St. This, despite the inexplicable change in its spelling, is named in honor of Methodist evangelist **George Whitefield** (1714–70), who crossed the Atlantic seven times to lead the frontier revival movement known as "The Great Awakening." The orphanage he founded at Savannah became Bethesda College.

Continue into Tottenham Court Rd., turn right and pause outside the curiously-named "Eisenhower Centre." Now used as a facility for security storage of documentation, this concrete bunker was originally a very deep, very large bomb-proof shelter which accommodated planning staff working on the D-Day invasion – which should surely explain its name.

Continue onwards to the American Church, which stands on the site of Whitefield's Tabernacle. Built for that charismatic preacher in 1756, the original chapel soon attracted such congregations that it had to be enlarged in 1759. After refurbishment and two rebuildings, it was destroyed by a V-bomb in 1945. (The whole road was pretty well devastated, as the number of rather uninspiring postwar buildings along the opposite side makes clear.) The church was rebuilt in the 1950s for the use of London's American community. Apart from welcoming all-comers to its non-sectarian worship, it also manages a very active outreach program among London's disadvantaged. The burial ground, now a public seating area, contains the remains of the **Reverend Augustus Toplady**, author of the American frontier's favorite anthem, *Rock of Ages.*

Turn right into Tottenham St. The Scala Theater which

The American Church on Tottenham Court Road. To the right, behind the trees, is the bomb-proof wartime bunker used by Eisenhower's planning staff. Behind looms the BT telecommunications tower.

formerly stood at Nos. 21–25, in 1911 became one of London's earliest cinemas and in 1915 screened D. W. Griffith's epoch-making epic of the American civil war, *Birth of a Nation*. In 1943, it served as the temporary home of the U.S. Army Theater Unit. Its memory is preserved only as the name of an exclusive apartment block. Between 1878 and 1902, the basement of No. 49 served as a meeting place for the Communist Working-Men's Club. Karl Marx (1818–83) and William Morris (1834–96) both lectured there.

At the end of Tottenham St. turn left back into Cleveland St. and cross Goodge St. to enter Newman St. From 1774 until his death, American artist **Benjamin West** (1738–1820) lived at No. 14 in a fine house with a charming garden and a lofty suite of painting rooms. As History Painter to King George III, West was well able to support such an establishment and a staff of five servants and to entertain such guests as Sir Joshua Reynolds, founder of the Royal Academy, whom West succeeded as President. West's artistic talent and social eminence made him the inevitable mentor of a school of young American painters, including Gilbert Stuart, John Trumbull, John Singleton Copley, Samuel Morse, and Charles Leslie, all of whom studied in his Newman Street atelier. Maintaining the painterly tradition, **Whistler** rented his first London studio at No. 70 in 1859. It was a dingy first-floor back room, with a remnant of silk drapery (it *would* be silk!) hung down the middle of the room to divide it into parlor and bedroom. One of Whistler's models, red-headed Joanna Hiffernan, daughter of an Irish laborer, soon rescued him from squalor by becoming his mistress and agent. Following his success at the 1860 Royal Academy Summer Exhibition, they moved from here to Paris in 1861.

Turn left through Newman Passage to emerge into Rathbone Street. Turn right and pause at the junction of Rathbone St., Charlotte St. and Percy St.

To the north, up Charlotte Street, you can see the Fitzroy Tavern, a favored haunt of such writers as **George Orwell, Evelyn Waugh, Dylan Thomas**, and 1927 Pulitzer Prize-winner **Thornton Wilder**. In Percy St. a blue plaque marks the former home of British-born Hollywood star **Charles Laughton** (1899–1962), who won an Oscar in 1932 for his performance in the title role of *The Private Life of Henry VIII* and became a U.S. citizen in 1950. In 1914, the White Tower restaurant (then known as the Tour Eiffel) was the scene of a celebratory meal for American-born poet-painter **Percy Wyndham Lewis** (1884–1957) (who lived at 4 Percy St.) and **Ezra Pound**, who had just launched a magazine - *Blast* - as the house journal of the avant-garde Vorticist movement. Vorticism, which flourished briefly between

1912 and 1915, attacked the alleged sentimentality of conventional art and instead celebrated energy, violence, and the cult of the machine. The Marquis of Granby pub dates from near the end of the lifetime of the Marquis of Granby (1721–70). His dashing cavalry charge against the French at Warburg in 1760 won a major victory and made him a popular hero. During the battle he lost both hat and wig but charged on regardless – hence the phrase "to go at it bald-headed," which is how he is invariably depicted on pub signs. The reason there are so many pubs named after this now-forgotten commander is that he was very generous to veterans who had served well under him, granting them a bounty – which they often used to set themselves up in retirement as publicans.

Turn into Rathbone Place. From 1769 onwards, a house which once stood at this end of the street was the occasional home of American scientist and spy **Edward Bancroft** (1744–1821). Bancroft's fluent French and friendship with Ben Franklin qualified him to translate secret correspondence between the American rebels and their French allies throughout the Revolutionary War. Bancroft, however, passed on to the British copies of everything that went through his hands – in return for a massive £1,000 a year pay-off and the promise of a Professorship (of Divinity!) at King's College (now Columbia University) once the British recaptured New York. That particular career move failed to work out, but Bancroft was given a generous pension until his death. His treachery remained an undisclosed secret until 1891.

Pause outside the Wheatsheaf pub, where in 1936 Bohemian portraitist **Augustus John** (1878–1961) introduced Welsh poet **Dylan Thomas** (1914–53) to his future wife, **Caitlin Macnamara**. Thomas's subsequent meteoric rise to fame was matched by an equally spectacular dive into alcoholism, leading to his early death in the course of an American lecture tour. Folk singer

Robert Zimmermann's admiration for the self-destructive bard inspired him to change his name to "Bob Dylan."

Continue south down Rathbone Place. This now undistinguished street numbers among its former residents the essayist **William Hazlitt**, sculptor **John Flaxman**, and painter **John Constable** (who also had a studio in Charlotte Street and was another of West's pupils.) At No. 27 the "Bluestockings," a formidable group of eighteenth-century female intellectuals, used to meet for tea and high-minded conversation. A century later, **Karl Marx** used to come to a gymnasium here to take fencing lessons.

At the bottom of Rathbone Place turn left onto Oxford Street and continue east to reach Tottenham Court Road station (Central and Northern lines). Walk ends.

En Route: Richard Recommends

Food and Drink

Charlotte St. is lined with restaurants, mostly Greek and Italian, but also Spanish and Nepali. Hanway St. has Japanese, Korean, Spanish, and Indian.

Public Toilets

Upper Regent St. (N of Oxford Circus station). Great Portland St. station.

Delays and Diversions

A visitor center is scheduled to open at Broadcasting House in 1996. Pollock's Toy Museum, 1 Scala St. (£) specializes in traditional dolls, train-sets, puppets, etc. All Saints, Margaret St. is William Butterfield's 1849 masterpiece, High Gothic at its most exuberant.

Shopping and Souvenirs

King's of Sheffield (Regent St., by Cavendish Place) stocks cutlery and silver plate from the home of both.

The BBC Shop (south of All Souls) has tapes and videos of classic radio and TV shows and language courses, plus badges, pens, tie-pins, hats, T-shirts with BBC insignia. SPCK Bookshop, Holy Trinity Church, Euston Rd. stocks religious books of all kinds. Nice Irma's (Goodge St. and Charlotte St.) has a range of "ethnic" textiles, ceramics, and ornaments.

8

The Quiet Quarter: Tottenham Court Road to Chancery Lane

This walk lets you combine a visit to the British Museum with an exploration of "intellectual London," the home of the "Bloomsbury Group" of writers and artists which revolved around novelist Virginia Woolf. Bloomsbury was virtually all grazing land until major building occurred between 1775 and 1850, largely at the initiative of successive Dukes of Bedford. The names of their family (Russell) and relatives (Gower, Montague) and estates (Woburn) provide many of the local street-names.

Starting Point – Tottenham Court Rd. station (Central and Northern lines)

Walk north along the west side of Tottenham Court Rd. and pause to look across the road at the building whose ground floor is now occupied by two tourist restaurants and a chemist's. The upper floors still show clearly that this was once a single, vast pub, the Horseshoe, claimed to have been the largest in London. (A carved horseshoe motif can still be seen on the upper facade.) The present building dates from 1875 but the original pub went back to at least 1623. In 1900, the Horseshoe advertised itself as one of nine London pubs offering real American-style cocktails – and one of only two with a real American barman to mix them.

Cross this busy road with care, turn right into Great Russell St. and pause at the junction with Adeline Place, which was once the home of writer **Mrs. Laetitia Bar-**

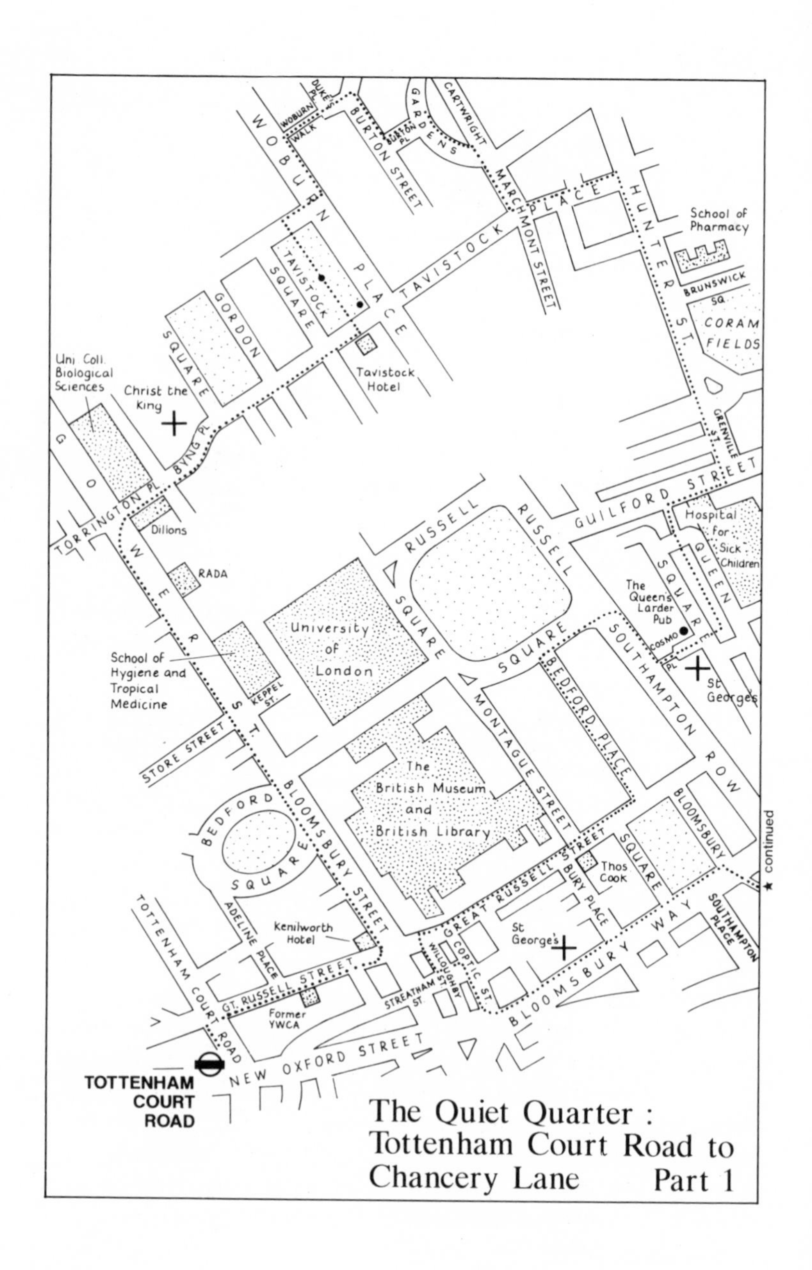

TOTTENHAM COURT ROAD
The Quiet Quarter : Tottenham Court Road to Chancery Lane Part 1
★ continued
University of London
The British Museum and British Library
School of Pharmacy
Coram Fields
Tavistock Hotel
Uni Coll. Biological Sciences
Christ the King
Dillons
RADA
School of Hygiene and Tropical Medicine
Hospital for Sick Children
The Queen's Larder Pub
St George's
Thos Cook
Kenilworth Hotel
Former YWCA

bauld (1743–1824), who in 1811 prophesied the rise of a wealthy and cultured America, from which one day visitors would come to survey "the grey ruin and the mouldering stone" of their ancestral homeland. A blue plaque at the end of the first block on the south side memorializes it as the supposed home of the Kitterbells, who figure in one of Dickens's earliest published sketches, *A Bloomsbury Christening*.

Continue eastwards to pass the former YWCA (now Central Club Hotel), designed by **Sir Edwin Lutyens** (1869–1944), the architect of the British Embassy in Washington and of the Cenotaph. *Note opposite* a bronze plaque marking the former home of **A. W. N. Pugin** (1812–52), co-architect of the Houses of Parliament. While living here as a youth he was designing scenery and stage machinery for the Theatre Royal, Drury Lane. *Further along the same side of the road is* Thanet House, the oldest building in Bloomsbury, dating from the 1680s and now a London base for Florida State University.

Continue to the junction of Great Russell St. with Bloomsbury St. American author Helen Hanff stayed at the Kenilworth Hotel here when visiting London to mark the publication of *84 Charing Cross Road*, which described her Platonic postal "affair" with English literature as supplied from that address. Hanff's book was later filmed, with Ann Bancroft and Sir Anthony Hopkins in the starring roles as author and bookseller. *Diagonally across the road you can see* a recently-built neo-Georgian red brick block. No. 6 Bloomsbury St. once stood here, housing the offices of poetry publisher **David Nutt**. In 1912, a frustrated and hesitant **Robert Frost** (1874–1963), having picked Nutt's name at random from the title-page of a book of verse, came here with the manuscript for his first volume of poems, *A Boy's Will*. Published by Nutt in 1913, it instantly made Frost's reputation and he returned to the States in triumph in 1915.

Walk left (north) along Bloomsbury St. into Bedford Square, the oldest (1775) complete square in London to survive virtually unaltered. The square was built as a residential area of the highest quality. (The 1861 census recorded a family of 13 at No. 6A - with 12 servants to wait on them.) No. 6 was the official home of the Lord Chancellor, the head of the English legal profession. Until the 1890s, gates barred the square to through traffic. Even after that it was still a highly desirable address and home to such grandees as ex-Prime Minister **Herbert Asquith**, architect **Sir Edwin Lutyens**, wealthy author **Sir Anthony Hope-Hawkins** (*The Prisoner of Zenda*), and the actor-manager **Sir Johnston Forbes-Robertson** (1853–1937). Since then the square has become synonymous with publishing. No. 8 long housed the offices of Frederick Warne and Co., publishers of Beatrix Potter. No. 11 was the home of **Henry Cavendish** (1731–1810), an eccentric millionaire recluse who was so shy that he communicated with his own servants by written notes. He was the first scientist to calculate the weight of the earth and discovered the chemical composition of both water and nitric acid. Cambridge University's world-famous Cavendish Laboratories are named in his honor.

Continue northwards, passing plaques which mark the homes of **Dame Millicent Garrett Fawcett** (1847–1929), non-violent campaigner for female suffrage, **Lady Ottoline Morrell** (1873–1938), society hostess, patroness (and occasional butt) of the "Bloomsbury Group" and **James Robinson** (1813–62), pioneer of anesthetic dentistry.

Pause at the first set of traffic lights and look left along Store St. In 1792, this was the home of **Mary Wollstonecraft** (1759–97), author of the first great feminist tract in English, *A Vindication of the Rights of Women.* Later that year she went to revolutionary Paris with an American, Gilbert Imlay, by whom she had a daughter, Fanny. Returning to London, she was twice driven to

The Senate House of the University of London. British TV programmakers have used it as a set to substitute for a 1920s New York skyscraper apartment block.

attempt suicide by Imlay's neglect and philandering. In 1797, she reluctantly bowed to convention and married radical William Godwin, only to die shortly after the birth of their child, Mary - who grew up to marry the poet Shelley and write *Frankenstein* (1818).

Look right along Keppel St. to see the towering bulk of the Senate House of the University of London. Completed just as World War Two broke out, it was said to have been built so high so that London students could look down on those of Oxford and Cambridge. It became the home of the Ministry of Information and thus a familiar haunt of American war correspondents. **George Orwell** (1903–50), a wartime broadcaster for the BBC, got his literary revenge by making it the model for the Stalinist "Ministry of Truth" in his *1984*, published in 1948. **Graham Greene**, for similar reasons, had already made it his "Ministry of Fear" in 1943. The building on the north side of Keppel St. is the London School of Hygiene and Tropical Medicine. In the 1920s, it was hoped to build a projected National Theatre here, but funds failed to materialize. In the event the site was bought for the University through the generosity of the Rockefeller Foundation.

Continue northwards and pause outside No. 52, where a plaque marks the site of the first operation in Europe to be performed under anesthetic, in 1846. Surgeon **Robert Liston**, who had witnessed the use of ether in Boston, Mass. earlier that same year, amputated a leg with his legendary swiftness and then turned to his admiring colleagues to announce triumphantly, "Gentlemen! This Yankee dodge beats Mesmerism!" (i.e., hypnotism). This remark was something of an in-joke, as the first Professor of Surgery at University College Hospital had lost his chair on account of his unsuccessful attempts to hypnotize patients into not feeling his scalpel.

A little further north pause outside the entrance to the Royal Academy of Dramatic Art, Britain's premier drama school, which was founded by such theatrical luminaries as Shaw (who bequeathed it a third of his royalties), J. M. Barrie, and Sir Johnston Forbes-Robertson. Its distinguished alumni include Hollywood stars Charles Laughton, seven times Oscar-nominated Peter O'Toole, and *Dynasty* star Joan Collins.

Continue northwards along Gower St. and pause by Dillon's bookshop. The gray stone building on the opposite side of the road to the north is the Biological Sciences block of University College and stands, very appropriately, on the first marital home of evolutionist **Charles Darwin** (1809–82). Darwin lived here after his return from his three-year round-the-world voyage aboard *HMS Beagle*. **Alexander Graham Bell** (1847–

1922), Scottish-born inventor of the telephone, lectured at University College on problems of speech and hearing.

Turn right past Dillon's and the cathedral-size University Church of Christ the King and pause to look left (south) to the lawn which is all that remains of Torrington Square. A bronze plaque on the one remaining terrace of houses on the east side records the home of usually neurotic, occasionally erotic, poet **Christina Rossetti** (1830–94); blighted in love and damaged in health, she seldom left her home or received visitors. Her most anthologized poems are, characteristically, "Up-hill" and "When I Am Dead."

Continue along the south side of Gordon Square, the most favored gathering-place of the "Bloomsbury Group." Plaques on its eastern terrace mark the homes of **J. M. Keynes** and of pacifist and iconoclastic biographer **Lytton Strachey** (1880–1932), who wrote brief, but exquisitely-phrased, muckraking lives of such Victorian icons as Florence Nightingale and General Gordon. At one Bloomsbury party guests were asked which character from history they would most like to have gone to bed with. Strachey opted for Julius Caesar.

Continue eastwards into Tavistock Square and pause by the Tavistock Hotel, which stands on the site of No. 52, where **Virginia Woolf** and her husband **Leonard** ran the Hogarth Press from 1924 until it was blitzed out. They concentrated on publishing new and experimental work and were the first to introduce the work of the American poets Jeffers, J. C. Ransom, and E. A. Robinson to English readers. T. S. Eliot's *The Waste Land* was printed here by them.

Cross into the gardens and note in the southeast corner the unusual double-sided statue honoring the redoubtable **Louisa Aldrich-Blake** (1865–1925), a pioneer surgeon and expert boxer! *In the middle of the gardens* another statue honors Indian independence leader **Mohandas Karamchand Gandhi** (1869–1948), who was

Pretty Woburn Walk, an 1820s gem, long home to W. B. Yeats.

once a law student in London. The cherry trees are a memorial to the victims of Hiroshima. *At the north end of the garden* a craggy rock serves as a memorial to conscientious objectors to military service. A blue plaque on the wall of the headquarters of the British Medical Association *on the east side of the square* records that **Charles Dickens's** last and most opulent London home once stood there. George Eliot recorded cattily that the luxuriously-fitted, deep-pile-carpeted library was an *entirely* appropriate setting for the labors of an author who sympathized *so* much with the sufferings of the poor. Nevertheless, Dickens wrote *Bleak House, Hard Times, Little Dorritt,* and *A Tale of Two Cities* while living here.

Leave the square by the northeast corner and walk up Upper Woburn Place to turn into Woburn Walk, a bijou shopping street dating from 1822. A bronze plaque at No. 5 shows where Nobel Prize-winning Irish poet and nationalist **W. B. Yeats** (1865–1939) lived for twenty years. **Ezra Pound** was a frequent guest here at Yeats's celebrated Monday evening gatherings. After Yeats left it his apartment was taken over by his great lost love **Maud Gonne.**

Leave Woburn Walk via Duke's Place to turn right into Burton St. and left via Burton Place into Cartwright Gardens, named in honor of the man whose statue stands with its back to you amid the trees and tennis courts. **John Cartwright** (1740–1824), having served with distinction in the navy and as chief magistrate of Newfoundland, became, as the inscription on the plinth of his memorial records, "the first English writer who openly maintained the independence of the United States of America" and, "Although his distinguished merits as a Naval Officer in 1776 presented the most flattering prospects of professional advancement yet he nobly refused to draw his Sword against the Rising Liberties of an oppressed and struggling people." Cartwright spent most of his later life agitating for a more democratic British constitution based on universal suffrage and annually elected parliaments. A brown plaque at the southeast corner of the square marks the former residence of **Sir Rowland Hill** (1795–1879). While living here in 1837, he wrote the pamphlet which argued for the introduction of cheap, universal pre-paid postage, based on his invention – the adhesive stamp. Realizing that the recent introduction of railways would render the horse-drawn stagecoach and its limited carrying-capacity utterly obsolete, Hill urged the abolition of charging postage according to distance. The "Penny Post" and the world's first stamps were introduced in 1840.

Walk south into Marchmont St., left into Tavistock Place and right into Hunter St. to enter Brunswick Sq. and pause opposite the road in front of the School of Pharmacy to see at the end of it the statue of **Captain Thomas Coram** (1668–1751). Coram spent more than a decade in Massachusetts, running shipyards in Boston and Taunton. Returning to London, he campaigned tirelessly for almost twenty years to establish the city's first orphan-

Kindly Captain Coram, founder of London's first orphanage. Notice its charter with the royal seal, in his right hand.

age for abandoned children. (Opposition focused on the curious argument that such an institution constituted a virtual incitement to promiscuity.) Eventually, the Foundling Hospital was established here in 1739 and here it remained until 1926. The area is still home to the Institute of Child Health and the Great Ormond Street Hospital for Sick Children, to which J. M. Barrie bequeathed the royalties from *Peter Pan* – worth tens of millions of pounds over the years. Coram Fields, the play area commemorating the kindly Captain, can only be entered by adults "if accompanied by a child." Hundreds of the orphans who "graduated" from the Foundling Hospital were sent to make new lives in the New World. Having arrived nameless in Brunswick

Square, many were given the family names of the Hospital's governors and benefactors, who came from the cream of London society and also included such celebrities as the composer Handel (hence nearby Handel St.) and the artists Hogarth and Reynolds. Some of the American descendants of the Foundling emigrants have subsequently returned, hoping to trace an aristocratic ancestry - only to discover their origins in a servant girl's shame.

Continue forwards past the roundabout into Grenville St., then right into Guilford St., then left through a passageway beside the Institute of Neurology into Queen Square. At the north end of its gardens stands a statue of **Queen Charlotte**, devoted consort of **George III**, the last royal ruler of America. As a result of an hereditary blood disease, porphyria, the king was subject to periodic bouts of insanity, brilliantly portrayed by Nigel Hawthorne in the film of Alan Bennett's play *The Madness of King George*. On one occasion he was brought here to the consulting rooms of his physician, Dr. Willis. Apart from subjecting the luckless king to numerous barbarities, Willis also attempted a more subtle therapy, persuading the dutiful Charlotte to prepare the king's favorite dishes in the hope that familiar food might somehow seduce him back to sanity. The ingredients were kept in store in the cellar of the pub on the western side of the square, now very appropriately known as the Queen's Larder.

Leave the square via Cosmo Place, the passageway between the Queen's Larder and St. George's church, and pause outside Peter's Bar to note the blue plaque recording the birthplace of **Sir John Barbirolli** (1899–1970), who succeeded Toscanini as conductor of the New York Philharmonic in 1937.

Turn right into Southampton Row and left into Russell Square, London's second largest square, laid out in 1805 by leading landscape architect **Humphrey Repton.** At that time it was one of the smartest addresses in the capital. Society portraitist **Sir Thomas Lawrence** had his studio where the Imperial Hotel now stands and **W. M. Thackeray** made it the fictional home of the vain and wealthy Osborne and Sedley families in his *Vanity Fair*. The plane trees are particularly fine, despite the devastation of the 1987 hurricane, which destroyed 15,000,000 trees throughout southern England. The plane, London's most common tree, is a hybrid of American and Asian varieties, first planted in the capital around 1680. **Edgar Allan Poe** (1809–49) lived in this square as a boy (1815–20) with his adoptive family, the Allans. **Ralph Waldo Emerson** lodged at No. 63 on his first visit to London in 1833. At the northwest corner of the square a brown plaque on No. 24 honors Nobel Prize-winner **T. S. Eliot**, who worked there for forty years for poetry publishers Faber and Faber. The statue on the south side of the square is of the fifth **Duke of Bedford**, whose agricultural interests are suggested by the plough-share, wheat-stook, sheep, etc. which complement his sturdy figure.

Leave Russell Sq. via Bedford Place, opposite the Duke's statue, to enter Bloomsbury Square. Laid out in the 1660s, this was the first London square actually to be called a square. **Gertrude Stein** (1874–1946) lived here briefly before moving on to a far more congenial exile in Paris. The statue of **Charles James Fox** is a fine historical mish-mash; clad in a Roman toga, he clutches a scroll – Magna Carta!

Turn right, passing the Paul Mellon Centre for Studies in British Art, which is attached to Yale University, and pause at the corner of Montague St. **Arthur Conan Doyle** (1859–1930) lodged at No. 23 when he first came to London, a less than successful doctor and still unknown as an author. The invitation came from a representative of the American publisher, Lippincott, who entertained him with another literary guest – **Oscar Wilde**. As a result of this momentous meal, Wilde wrote *The Picture of Dorian Grey* and Doyle *The Sign of*

An aerial view of the British Museum in the inter-war period. The Senate House of the University of London (completed 1940) has not yet been built and the area is still occupied by allotments (vegetable gardens) established by policemen from the station in Tottenham Court Road during World War One.

Four. Sherlock Holmes's earliest address was therefore Montague St., only later to be succeeded by the far more famous, but mythical, 221b Baker St.. The building on the other side of the road, at the corner of Bury Place, was in the 1860s the first London office of **Thomas Cook**, which also offered board and lodging to visitors. This was a shrewdly-chosen site, opposite what is still London's greatest indoor attraction, the British Museum, now pulling in 6,000,000 visitors a year. When Cook and his son began to make reservations at other establishments to deal with surplus customers, they took the decisive step which transformed them from mere sellers of train tickets to full-blown travel agents. In 1827, **John James Audubon** took lodgings at No. 55 while he scoured London to find an engraver for his definitive series of pictures of American birds. Audubon detested the gulf between rich and poor in London and found only sparrows in Great Russell St., but London had more and better engravers in a single street than there were in all Philadelphia and he soon found that a dawn walk in Regent's Park lifted his soul for the day ahead. Audubon found his engraver, **Robert Havell**, at 79 Newman St. The eventual success of *Birds of America* immortalized Audubon's name and enabled Havell to graduate to an Oxford St. address.

Continue eastwards along Great Russell St. and pause to note a blue plaque at No. 46, once the residence of artist **Randolph Caldecott** (1846–86), who made his name with his illustrations for an 1875 edition of Washington Irving's *Sketch Books*. Acting on strict medical advice, the frail Caldecott took a trip to Florida for his health – and died of a fever within weeks, aged just 39.

Continue to the corner of Willoughby St. and pause to note No. 38, once the Poetry Bookshop run by Harold Monro. Robert Frost unobtrusively gatecrashed the opening party soon after arriving in England, but was given away by his distinctively American "wingtip" shoes. On the opposite side of the road a blue plaque at first-floor level marks the former home (1863–8) of artist-writer **George Du Maurier** (1834–96), who, as an impoverished art student in his native Paris, shared rooms with Whistler. A highly successful illustrator, he had to turn to writing as his sight began to fail. Drawing on his Bohemian youth for background, Du Maurier found belated fame with *Trilby* (1894), the story of a girl hypnotized by the evil Svengali into becoming a world-class opera singer. As a novel and a play (and a hat) *Trilby* took London by storm but the rewards came too late for Du Maurier. His younger son, the suave actor **Sir George Du Maurier** (1873–1934) first found fame as *Raffles: The Gentleman Thief*. His granddaughter Dame **Daphne Du Maurier** (1907–89) was the author of such bestselling romantic novels as *Jamaica Inn* (1936) and *Rebecca* (1938).

Walk south down Willoughby St. and pause in Streatham St. The new building on the north side, to your right, stands on the site of the Bloomsbury Dispensary where **Edward Jenner** (1749–1823) inaugurated the world's first systematic vaccination campaign against smallpox. Within five years of his discovery (1796), vaccination was saving lives in the remote backwoods of Kentucky and Tennessee, thanks to the London sojourn of **Benjamin Silliman** (see p. 55).

Turn left along Streatham Street and right into Coptic Street and pause to look along Little Russell Street, once the home of poet **W. H. Davies** (1871–1940), whose experiences as a hobo in America lost him a leg but won him fame when, with the encouragement of G. B. Shaw, he wrote them up as *The Autobiography of a Super-Tramp*.

Turn left at the bottom into Bloomsbury Way and pause outside St. George's church. Designed by **Nicholas Hawksmoor**, Wren's greatest pupil, it was completed in 1731. The extraordinary tower is modeled on Pliny's description of the Mausoleum of Halicarnassus, one of the Seven Wonders of the ancient world. (Whatever the mausoleum looked like it almost certainly wasn't like that, as you can see by checking in the appropriate gallery of the British Museum.) The statue on the top is **George I** (reigned 1714–27), the first of the Hanoverian line. Wits rhymed that:

> When Henry VIII left the Pope in the lurch,
> The Protestants made him head of the church,
> But George's good subjects, the Bloomsbury people,
> Instead of the Church, made him head of the steeple.

In 1913, a solemn funeral service was held here, attended by huge crowds of suffragettes, for **Emily Davison** (1872–1913), who had died after flinging herself at the King's horse during the Derby a few days before, to protest the cause of "Votes for Women!".

Continue along Bloomsbury Way into Bloomsbury Square. A plaque on the west side marks the former home of writer **Isaac D'Israeli** (1766–1848), father of **Benjamin Disraeli** (1804–81), Britain's only Jewish

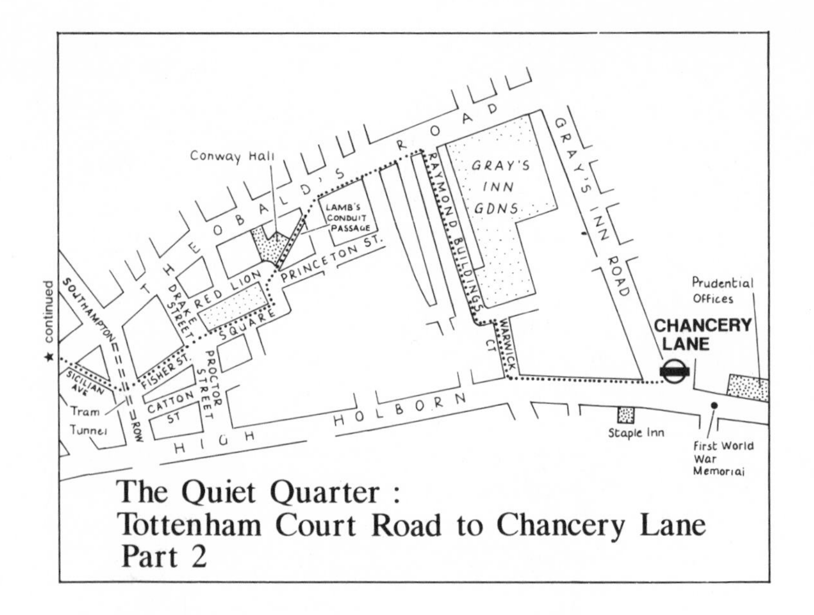

The Quiet Quarter : Tottenham Court Road to Chancery Lane Part 2

Prime Minister to date, who kept one step ahead of his creditors by writing bestsellers. Southampton Place to the right was the birthplace of **Cardinal Henry Newman** (1801–90), a leading figure in the nineteenth-century Catholic revival and author of *Lead, Kindly Light.* A bronze plaque on the south side of the square marks the former home of the fourth **Earl of Chesterfield** (1694–1773), a diplomat and politician renowned for suavity and elegance. His *Letters* to his (illegitimate) son were published posthumously as a handbook of gentlemanly behavior. He is also remembered, however, for having failed to respond to Dr. Johnson's request for support for his Dictionary project. When Chesterfield later wrote a favorable review of this great work, Johnson sent him a rebuke of crushing severity and later dismissed the *Letters* as teaching "the manners of a dancing-master and the morals of a whore."

Sicilian Avenue to Chancery Lane

Turn right into charming Sicilian Avenue and pause at the end to note the disused tram tunnel in the middle of Southampton Row. During World War Two, the Elgin (Parthenon) Marbles were hidden down here to protect them from bombs. On the opposite side of the road, on Baptist Church House at the corner of Catton Street, note a statue of tinker-preacher **John Bunyan** (1628–88), author of *The Pilgrim's Progress.*

Cross busy Southampton Row with care and walk through Fisher St. to cross Procter St. and enter Red Lion Square, built by the notorious speculator **Dr. Nicholas Barbon** in the 1680s. An exuberant statue at the western end of the gardens commemorates militant pacifist **Fenner Brockway** (1888–1988), while a more sober bust at the other end honors philosopher (and philanderer) **Bertrand Russell** (1872–1970), who won the Nobel Prize for Literature in 1950. A plaque on No. 8 marks the home of poet-painter **Dante Gabriel Rossetti** (1828–82), charismatic founder of the Pre-Raphaelite Brotherhood. This was later the home of his acolytes **William Morris** and **Edward Burne-Jones** (1833–98). The two young men, just down from Oxford, lived in amiable squalor as they flung themselves into art and craft-work. Morris's first effort was a huge settle which proved too big to get upstairs into their rooms. Princeton St. at the eastern end of the square was once Prince's St. and had its name amended just to to distinguish it from the many others bearing that name. At the northeast corner of the square stands Conway Hall, named in honor of **Moncure Daniel Conway** (1832–1907), a Virginian abolitionist who came to London to preach about the American civil war and stayed on for the next thirty years as a Unitarian pastor. His seventy books include a two-volume biography of Tom Paine.

Leave the square via Lamb's Conduit Passage and turn right along Theobald's Rd and right along Raymond's

Gray's Inn Dining Hall. Bombed out in the Blitz and refurbished through Canadian generosity.

Buildings to enter Gray's Inn, the northernmost of the four Inns of Court. Shakespeare's *Comedy of Errors* was first staged in the Hall here in 1594. The chapel, dating back to 1315, was destroyed by enemy bombing in 1941; the new pulpit, lectern, and pews are of maple, presented by the Canadian Bar Association. The fine gardens and gravel walks were laid out by **Francis Bacon** (1561–1626), whose statue can be seen in the Inn's South Square, where teenage **Charles Dickens** once worked rather miserably as a lawyer's clerk. Dickens soon got his revenge in *Pickwick Papers* in creating the character of Mr. Phunky, a junior counsel. Bacon, a philosopher and experimental scientist as well as lawyer, rose to become Lord Chancellor before being disgraced on charges of corruption. Ardent Baconites believe him to be the true author of Shakespeare's plays.

Leave via Warwick Court where a bronze plaque marks the site of the lodgings occupied by **Dr. Sun Yat-Sen** (Sun Yixian) (1866–1925), "father of modern China." Educated in Hawaii and Hong Kong, he spent

Staple Inn. The timbered facade dates from 1586. Originally the complex was a wool warehouse for merchants of the Staple (a trading association). In 1529, it was acquired by Gray's Inn and became an Inn of Chancery, serving as a preparatory institution for students before they graduated to an Inn of Court. Dr. Johnson lodged here in 1759.

much of his life in exile. During his stay in London he was kidnapped by staff of the Chinese legation and released on the intervention of the Foreign Office, an incident which catapulted him from obscurity to international notoriety.

Turn left onto High Holborn and pause to admire, on the opposite side of the street, the five-gabled half-timbered sixteenth-century facade of Staple Inn, once a wool warehouse and later a training center for lawyers. The impressive statue in the middle of the road is a memorial to the World War One dead (over 22,000) of the City of London's own regiment, the Royal Fusiliers. The neo-Gothic red brick Prudential Insurance headquarters designed by Alfred Waterhouse stands on the former site of Furnivall's Inn, where Dickens had rooms as a bachelor. A small bust of the author stands at the northwest corner of its inner courtyard.

Walk ends at Chancery Lane station (Central line).

Dickens' last surviving London home – at 48 Doughty St.

En Route: Richard Recommends

Food and Drink

There are cafés in the University Church of Christ the King (Gordon Sq.) and the British Museum, in Woburn Walk and in Marchmont St. Southampton Row offers Italian, French, and Indian restaurants. Wagamama is a Japanese noodle bar (Streatham St.). "Character" pubs include the Museum Tavern (Great Russell St.), Queen's Larder (Queen Sq.), the Enterprise (Red Lion St.), the Sun (Lamb's Conduit St.), and the Princess Louise (High Holborn).

Public Toilets

Underpass leading into Tottenham Court Rd. station.

Russell Square (NE corner, by Woburn Place). (Not exactly public but readily accessible are those in the basement at the British Museum.)

Delays and Diversions

The Percival David Foundation, 53 Gordon Square is one of the world's great collections of Chinese ceramics. The British Museum defies superlatives - and is still free. Display cases in the King's Library house not only autograph manuscripts by Shakespeare and Dickens (and John Lennon) but also two of the four surviving original copies of Magna Carta and two letters to double agent Sir George Downing. There is also a letter from George III, dated March 1777, urging his generals to abandon any "hearts and minds" campaign and get tough with the American rebels because "the regaining their affection is an idle idea, it must be convincing them that it is their interest to submit and then they will dread further broils." Dickens' House, 48 Doughty Street (£) is the only one of his ten London homes to survive, stuffed with memorabilia, original furnishings, and editions of his work.

Shopping and Souvenirs

The British Museum has an excellent bookshop; also gifts, such as jewelry based on famous exhibits. The area is rich in bookshops, focusing on specialist interests, such as film, North Africa, the occult, and medical history. Westaway and Westaway (Bloomsbury St. and Great Russell St.) specialize in woolens and "typically British" garments. Cosmo Place Studio (Cosmo Place) specializes in hand-painted ceramics. The Bloomsbury Workshop, 12 Galen Place (off Pied Bull Yard, off Bury Place) specializes in prints and books by and about the "Bloomsbury Group." Photographic "bygones" are the stock-in-trade of the Rare Camera Company and Jessop Classic Photographica, both of Pied Bull Yard. Gosh at 39 Great Russell St. is for comic book freaks. On New

Oxford St., James Smith & Sons at No. 53 make and sell umbrellas, whips, shooting-sticks, etc. At No. 45 nearby Creativity is a must for embroidery and knitting fans. The Tibet Shop at 10 Bloomsbury Way is just what its name says it is. The Silver Vaults (off Chancery Lane) are an underground treasure house of the silversmith's art. One block east of Chancery Lane station is Hatton Garden, London's gold and jewelry district.

9

Little America: Marble Arch to Hyde Park Corner

Some parts of London, like Fitzrovia, start out classy and go downmarket. Mayfair started classy and stayed that way. This golden rectangle, almost entirely built up between 1700 and 1750, is inhabited primarily by diplomats and the very rich; the British, in other words, are thin on the ground. Along our route we will pass Embassy or High Commission properties belonging to the United States, Canada, Italy, Myanmar (Burma), the Bahamas, Mexico, and Tanzania. We will also pass the windows of some *very* exclusive shops.

Starting Point - Marble Arch station (Central line)
Leave the station via exit no. 2 and pause at the top of the stairs to look over towards Marble Arch itself. Designed by **John Nash** and modeled on the Arch of Constantine in Rome, the Arch was originally erected in front of Buckingham Palace in 1827, but moved to its present location in 1851 and was turned into a traffic island in 1908. It stands on the site of Tyburn, London's principal execution site from 1388 until 1783. The triangular gallows could accommodate 21 criminals at a time and was noted in a 1740s guidebook as a visitor attraction well worth checking out. *Beyond Marble Arch, stretching away to the west is* Bayswater Rd., where, at Tyburn convent, prayers are said daily for the souls of Catholics martyred at Tyburn between 1558 and 1681. On Bayswater Rd., in 1861 an American entrepreneur, appropriately named Mr. Train, tried to inaugurate

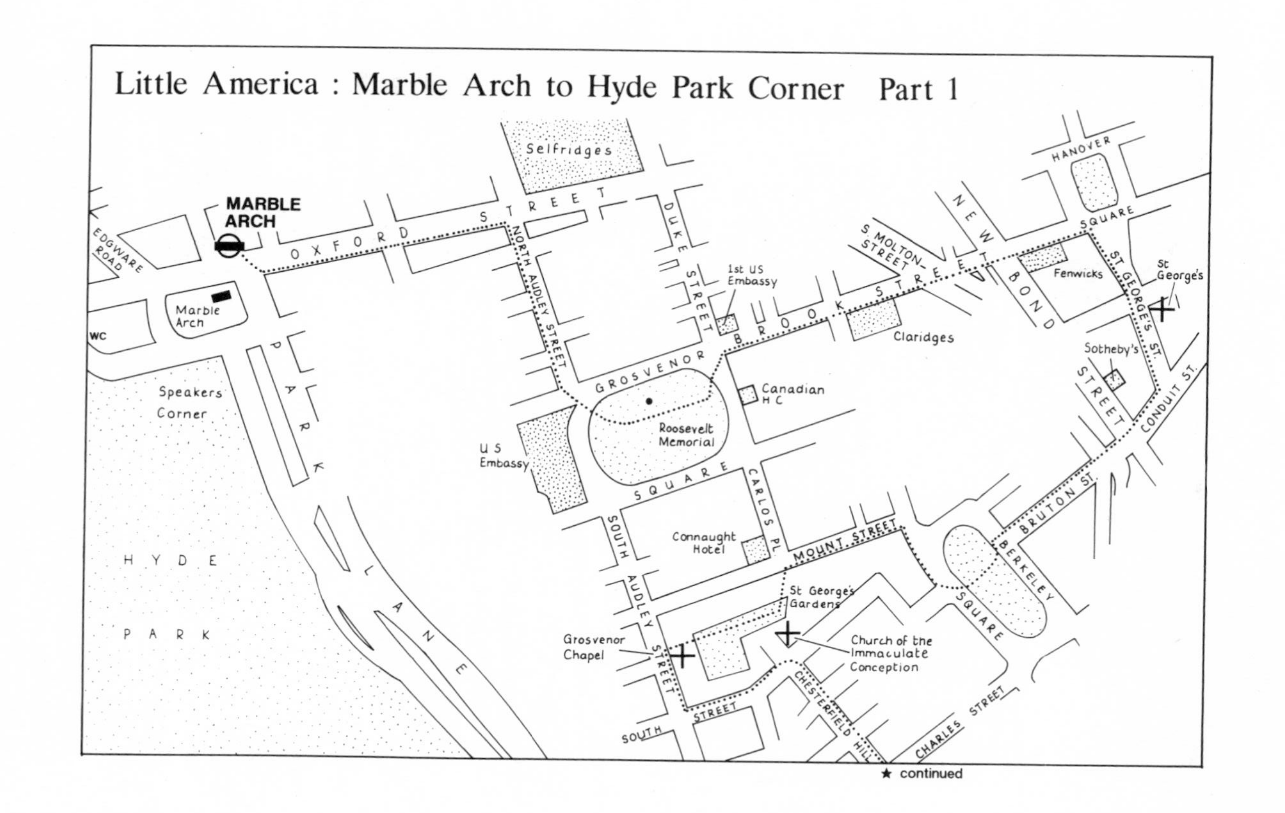
Little America : Marble Arch to Hyde Park Corner Part 1
MARBLE ARCH
EDGWARE ROAD
Marble Arch
WC
Speakers Corner
HYDE PARK
PARK LANE
OXFORD STREET
Selfridges
NORTH AUDLEY STREET
DUKE STREET
1st US Embassy
BROOK STREET
S. MOLTON-STREET
NEW BOND
Fenwicks
HANOVER SQUARE
ST GEORGE'S ST.
St George's
Sotheby's
STREET
CONDUIT ST.
Claridges
GROSVENOR SQUARE
Canadian HC
Roosevelt Memorial
US Embassy
CARLOS PL
Connaught Hotel
MOUNT STREET
SOUTH AUDLEY STREET
St George's Gardens
Grosvenor Chapel
Church of the Immaculate Conception
CHESTERFIELD HILL
SOUTH STREET
CHARLES STREET
BERKELEY SQUARE
BRUTON ST.
★ continued

Marble Arch *c.*1908

London's first horse-drawn tram service. *To the left of Marble Arch, at the northeast corner of Hyde Park, is* Speaker's Corner, where you may denounce or pronounce as you wish, providing you stand on something to do so. *To the right of Marble Arch, at the corner of Edgware Road,* a blue plaque on a cream-stuccoed mansion marks it as the former home of **Lord Randolph Churchill**, Sir Winston's father.

Turn left into Oxford St., Europe's longest shopping street, walk eastwards and pause at the corner of North Audley St. to look at Selfridges. **Gordon Selfridge** (1864–1947) had already made himself a millionaire in Chicago before he opened his state-of-the-art London store in 1909. **Daniel Burnham** of Chicago was the consulting architect for this monumental pile. Selfridge was the first retailer to promote the idea of shopping as an "experience" and appealed to his customers to "Spend the Day at Selfridge's," where a lady from out of town could buy everything she wanted and have lunch, get her hair done, etc. Selfridge eventually fell under the thrall of a pair of cabaret dancers, twin sisters who fleeced him of £2,000,000 and left him

Ike.

dependent on the charity of his daughter. *On the south side of the road the second shop from the corner was once* the main retail outlet for designer **William Morris.** Morris's chief furniture-maker was an American, George Washington Jack, and from the 1880s onwards Morris did a thriving export business through a Boston agent.

Walk down North Audley St to enter Grosvenor Square (1720s) by a statue of **Eisenhower**, a gift from his home state of Kansas. Behind him looms the U.S. Embassy, designed by Finnish-American **Eero Saarinen**; completed in 1959, it is the largest in Britain. *The block to your left bears a plaque marking it as* one of the many buildings occupied by Ike's staff.

Cross into Grosvenor Square to see an imposing statue of **Franklin Delano Roosevelt**, unveiled by his widow

FDR.

in 1948, the cost having been raised by public subscription in the UK in a matter of a few days. *Opposite FDR stands* an obelisk surmounted by an eagle, which commemorates the men of the American Eagles squadrons which flew with the RAF from the outbreak of war in 1939 until they were integrated with the USAF in September 1942.

Leave the square by the northwest corner and pause at the junction with Duke St. before you cross the road. *To your right* No. 7 was the former residence of **Walter Hines Page**, Anglophile U.S. Ambassador during World War One. *To its right* a former U.S. Embassy building is now occupied by the Canadian High Commission. *To the left* No. 9 at the junction of Duke St. and Brook St. bears a plaque marking it as the very first U.S. Embassy, occupied by John Adams from 1785 onwards.

Enter Brook St., which takes its name from the Tyburn, one of London's "lost rivers," which cuts across it underground. Immediately to your right, at No. 75 is the office of the Anglo-American Chamber of Commerce, established in 1916 - a significant gesture of confidence at a dark hour, which must have owed much to the influence of Ambassador Page. No. 76, opposite, was the home of **Colen Campbell** (1676-1729), yet another ambitious Scot who migrated profitably to London after the Act of Union between England and Scotland in 1707 and designed the first houses to be built on the eastern side of Grosvenor Square. His influential treatise *Vitruvius Britannicus* was *the* source for all smitten with the craze for Palladian architecture. No. 74 was the home of Queen Victoria's physician, **Sir William Gull**, one of many suspects for the murders committed by "Jack the Ripper." At No. 68, a few doors along, OSS (Office of Strategic Services), wartime forerunner of the CIA, had its headquarters. Claridges, designed by the man who also designed Harrod's (and doesn't it look it?), is London's most exclusive hotel, where royals and presidents often stay on for a few days after a state visit. **Scott** and **Zelda Fitzgerald** stayed here in 1921 and were entertained by Churchill's mother who lived at No. 72 and gave them "strawberries as big as tomatoes." **William J. Donovan**, head of OSS, lived at Claridges and so did **Harry Hopkins**, when he came secretly in January 1941 as FDR's personal envoy. He initiated the Lend-Lease program, which he was to administer, delivering vital armaments to Britain in another hour of direst need. Later occupants included **Generals Eisenhower, Clark**, and **Marshall**. No. 39 was once the home of **Sir Jeffrey Wyatville** (1766-1840), who gothicized Windsor Castle for George IV. Colefax & Fowler, who occupy the ground floor, pioneered the English "country house" style of interior decor. At No. 25 **Handel** (1685-1759) composed "Messiah" in just three weeks. Rock guitarist **Jimi Hendrix** once briefly lived in the next-door house. *Notice how, at this point, the neat right-angle layout of streets is cut across by the diagonal of* South Moulton St., which follows the line of the Tyburn.

Cross Bond St., London's most expensive shopping thoroughfare, where naval hero **Admiral Lord Nelson** lived at No. 106 in 1798, *and continue eastwards to pause at the corner of* Hanover Square, dominated by a statue of **Pitt the Younger**. A plaque at the eastern end of Brook St. marks the former residence of that great political survivor and arch-cynic **Prince Talleyrand**, who managed to serve every French regime from the revolutionary 1790s through to the royalist 1830s. (Motto: "Distrust first impulses, they are nearly always good") The modern block on the eastern side of the square occupies the site of historic concert rooms where J. C. Bach, Liszt, and Wagner all once performed. Senator **Daniel Webster** stayed at the Brunswick House Hotel, on the site of No. 10, in 1839, when his daughter Julia was married in St. George's Church just off the square. Carlyle, who breakfasted with Webster and Wordsworth, wrote enthusiastically to Emerson of the impression "the notablest of all your Notabilities" had made.

Turn right into Saint George St., where at No. 17 a bronze plaque records that **William Morris** founded "The Firm" in 1861 "for the advancement of his great reform in all the decorative arts." At No. 8 in 1860, during an Anglo-French war scare the socially exclusive Artists' Rifles was established as a volunteer militia. St. George's, the parish church for Mayfair, was built in 1724. Handel had a personal pew here and there is an altar painting of *The Last Supper*, probably by William Kent. Teddy Roosevelt, Shelley, Disraeli, George Eliot, and John Buchan were all married here, as was Prime Minister Asquith, with four other past or future premiers in the congregation.

At the bottom turn right into Conduit St. and cross into Bruton St. Walk along the north side which is lined with art dealers. *On the opposite side of the road* a plaque at No. 17 marks where HM **Queen Elizabeth II** was born on April 21, 1926 in the London home of her maternal grandfather, the Earl of Strathmore. As her father was not at that time expected to become king there was little concern when her birthplace was demolished to make way for a car showroom (although it *is* a Rolls-Royce dealership).

Cross into Berkeley Square, where the huge and handsome plane trees date from *c.*1789. Berkeley Square House on the east side of the square housed the first offices of SOE (Special Operations Executive), the sabotage organization created by Churchill to "set Europe ablaze." To the south once stood Lansdowne House, an Adam mansion of 1762, where Joseph Priestley, then its librarian, discovered oxygen. It was later the home of **Waldorf Astor** and, after him, of **Gordon Selfridge**. Its dining room is now in the Metropolitan Museum, New York and its drawing room in the Philadelphia Museum of Art. When No. 45 was newly built it was occupied by the fabulously wealthy but melancholic **Robert Clive**, who began the British conquest of India but committed suicide here. No. 44, designed by **William Kent** (1744), is said to be the finest terraced house in London; its sumptuous interior, which impressed even the snooty connoisseur **Horace Walpole** who once lived opposite, now houses a private gambling club and a jet-set disco. No. 40 was where many OSS agents were briefed before going on operations; the Americans came late to the espionage game and initially followed the British pattern of recruitment, selecting maverick types with an Ivy League background.

Leave the Square by the northwest corner to enter Mount St. and pass a hairdresser's whose clients include **Princess Diana** (she probably doesn't have to book

The most perfect terraced house in London? 44 Berkeley Square.

three months ahead but lesser mortals do), also a wonderful florist's and a remarkable butcher's shop. *On the opposite side of the road is* the Connaught Hotel, which specializes in discreet luxury for celebs with a Garbo complex who really do want privacy. Until World War One it was called the Coburg but that sounded too German and the switch to Connaught saved having to alter the monograms on cutlery, linen, etc. (For the same reason George V changed the royal family name from Saxe-Coburg-Gotha to Windsor.) Carlos Place is where **Oscar Wilde** stayed on returning from lecturing Colorado miners on aesthetics, immortalizing his experiences in the arch *Impressions of America* (1883).

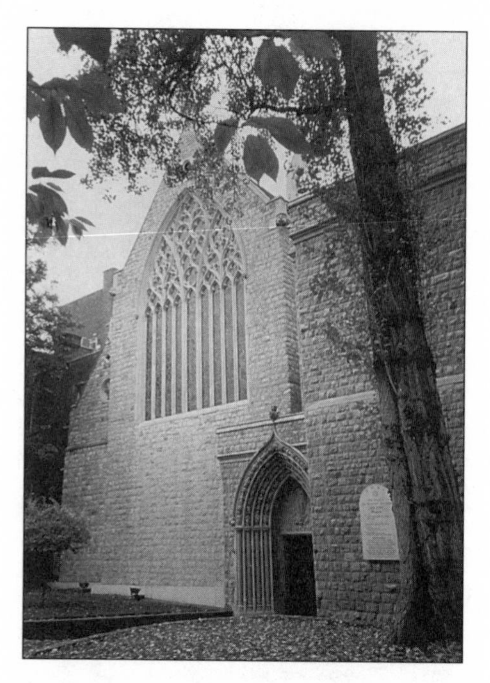

The Church of the Immaculate Conception, Farm St., as seen from St. George's Gardens.

Turn left and go through the gates into St. George's Gardens. More than two dozen of the benches here have been donated by Americans and Canadians who loved its calm atmosphere. Ironically, they were also used by KGB agents to pass coded messages to local contacts by means of chalk-marks or thumb-tacks. You *must*, if there is no service on, go into the Church of the Immaculate Conception (1844), home to England's Jesuits. The altar, by **Pugin**, is simply breathtaking.

Leave St George's Gardens to enter South Audley St. just by the Grosvenor Chapel (1730), which was the American forces' chapel during World War Two. Its fashionable congregation has included **Lady Mary Wortley Montagu**, who brought back the secret of inoculation against smallpox from Turkey in the 1720s; radical **John Wilkes**, in his respectable old age; **Florence Nightingale**; and former Poet Laureate **John Betjeman**, who called it "a little piece of New England in warm old London brick." The cool, serene interior is a marked contrast to the gloomy grandeur of the Immaculate Conception. On the opposite side of the road is Purdey's, doyen of gunmakers, where a pair of shotguns will set you back $100,000.

Pass the stunning window displays of china and glass specialist Thos. Goode & Co. to turn left into South St., where No. 15 was home to **Catherine Walters** from 1872 until her death in 1920. A skilled and spirited horsewoman who rode daily in nearby Hyde Park, this most notorious of courtesans was universally known as "Skittles" and numbered the future Edward VII among her many lovers.

Chesterfield Hill to Hyde Park Corner

Take the second right down Chesterfield Hill and turn right into Charles St. **Lord Rosebery**, who once occupied No. 20, left Oxford without a degree to devote himself to horse-racing and was far more proud of having his horses win the Derby three times than he was of becoming Prime Minister. At No. 22 William IV, when still only **Duke of Clarence**, lived in domestic bliss with his doting mistress, the talented actress, **Mrs. Jordan**. On ascending the throne, however, the "Sailor King," unceremoniously dumped her and their numerous offspring, leaving her to die in poverty and obscurity.

Turn left into Chesterfield St., where novelist **William Somerset Maugham** once lived at No. 6 and the dandy **Beau Brummell** lived at No. 4. It was in this house allegedly that the Prince Regent burst into tears when the arbiter of fashion damned the cut of his coat.

Turn left into Curzon St. and pause to admire Crewe House, built around 1730 by speculative developer

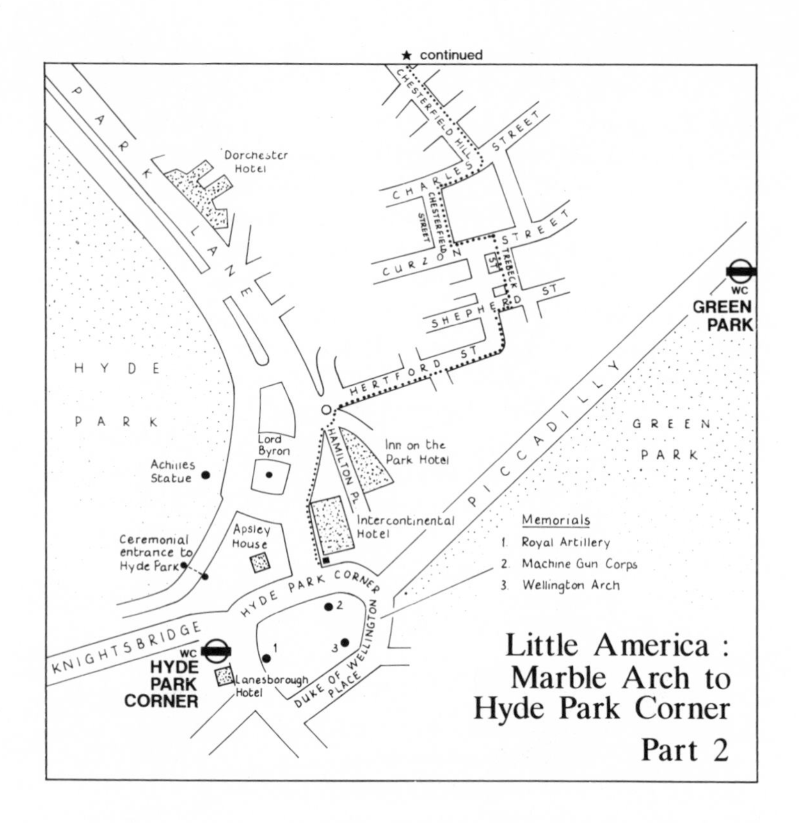

Edward Shepherd and refaced and extended in 1813. It is the sole survivor of the grand, detached residences characteristic of Mayfair's early development.

Cross into Trebeck St, where a plaque marks the site of the original two-week-long "Mayfair" which was transferred here from Haymarket in 1686 but abolished when its disorder and criminality became too tiresome for the local upper crust. The name of Tiddy Dol's restaurant recalls one of the fair's more colorful characters, a bizarrely dressed seller of gingerbread.

At the bottom turn right into Shepherd St. and follow it round into Hertford St. No. 10 was occupied by Swiss painter **Angelica Kauffman**, one of the 40 founders of the Royal Academy, then by two dramatists, **General John Burgoyne** (of Saratoga fame) and parliamentarian **Richard Brinsley Sheridan**, playwright of *The School for Scandal* and *The Rivals*. Sheridan opposed Britain's war with the American colonies so outspokenly that the Continental Congress offered him a reward - which he declined. He also took over the Theatre Royal, Drury Lane from Garrick and rebuilt it magnificently, only to have it burn down in 1809. When the news was brought to him in the House of Commons, Sheridan calmly finished making his speech, then went to the scene and took a relaxed drink in a nearby pub. Upbraided by onlookers for his phlegmatic reaction, Sheridan turned on them with the words "Can't a fellow take a glass in peace beside his own fire?"

Continue along Hertford St. At Stanhope Row, a turning to the right, a plaque marks the former site of "The Cottage," the oldest recorded building in this area, dating from 1618. No. 20 was once the home of **Sir George Cayley** (1773–1857), who beat the Wright brothers by the best part of a century when he launched a ten-year-old boy into flight on a glider of his design.

Enter Park Lane. To your right is the luxurious Dorchester Hotel, owned by the Sultan of Brunei. Go to your left, passing, marooned by the traffic, a statue of the poet **Byron** and his pet dog. *Beyond it, in Hyde Park, you should be able to make out* the colossal figure of Achilles, London's first nude statue, a tribute to the Duke of Wellington from the women of England. They didn't know that that was what they had been subscribing for, and a fig-leaf was added to it later.

Pass the Inn on the Park hotel, where eccentric billionaire **Howard Hughes** lived in seclusion in 1972–3, and *negotiate the complexities of the underpass system to emerge* on the green at Hyde Park Corner, which is dominated by memorials to the Machine Gun Corps

Hyde Park Corner c.1905. This actual postcard carried greetings from the then Grand Duke of Luxembourg.

(note the chilling quotation from the *Psalms*) and the Royal Artillery (quotation from Shakespeare's *Henry V*). **Wellington**, on his favorite mount, Copenhagen, faces the residence given to him by a grateful nation for defeating Napoleon at Waterloo, when the "Iron Duke" had less than nine hours sleep in the course of the four-day battle. Apsley House (by **Robert Adam**, 1771) rejoices in an address of sneering superiority - No. 1 London. Beside it the ceremonial entrance to Hyde Park, designed by **Decimus Burton**, bears a frieze, based on the Parthenon marbles, like the one on the Athenaeum (see p. 167). The arch behind Wellington's statue shows Peace descending into the chariot of Victory. The Lanesborough Hotel was originally St. George's Hospital, designed in the 1820s by **William Wilkins**, architect of the National Gallery.

Walk Ends. Depart via Hyde Park Corner station (Piccadilly line). Green Park station (Victoria, Jubilee, and Piccadilly lines) is only a short walk away through Green Park.

En Route: Richard Recommends

Food and Drink

Numerous eating places line Oxford St. and North Audley St. but Shepherd Market has a couple of dozen in a pleasant villagey atmosphere. If you feel like treating yourself, Scott's (20 Mount Street) is very English and has long been celebrated for its fish dishes. Look out for the 1937 menu signed by Clark Gable and Marlene Dietrich. The Hard Rock Café is near the end of the walk, on Piccadilly.

Public Toilets

Hyde Park Corner, west of Apsley House.

Delays and Diversions

Apsley House (£), a museum devoted to Wellington, recently sumptuously refurbished. Exhibits include **Canova's** monumental statue of **Napoleon**, portraits of **Wellington** by **Goya** and **Lawrence**, numerous Old Masters, and a stupendous Sèvres dinner service ordered by Napoleon as a *divorce* present for Josephine.

Shopping and Souvenirs

If you can afford to shop around here you don't need my suggestions. Otherwise just *look*.

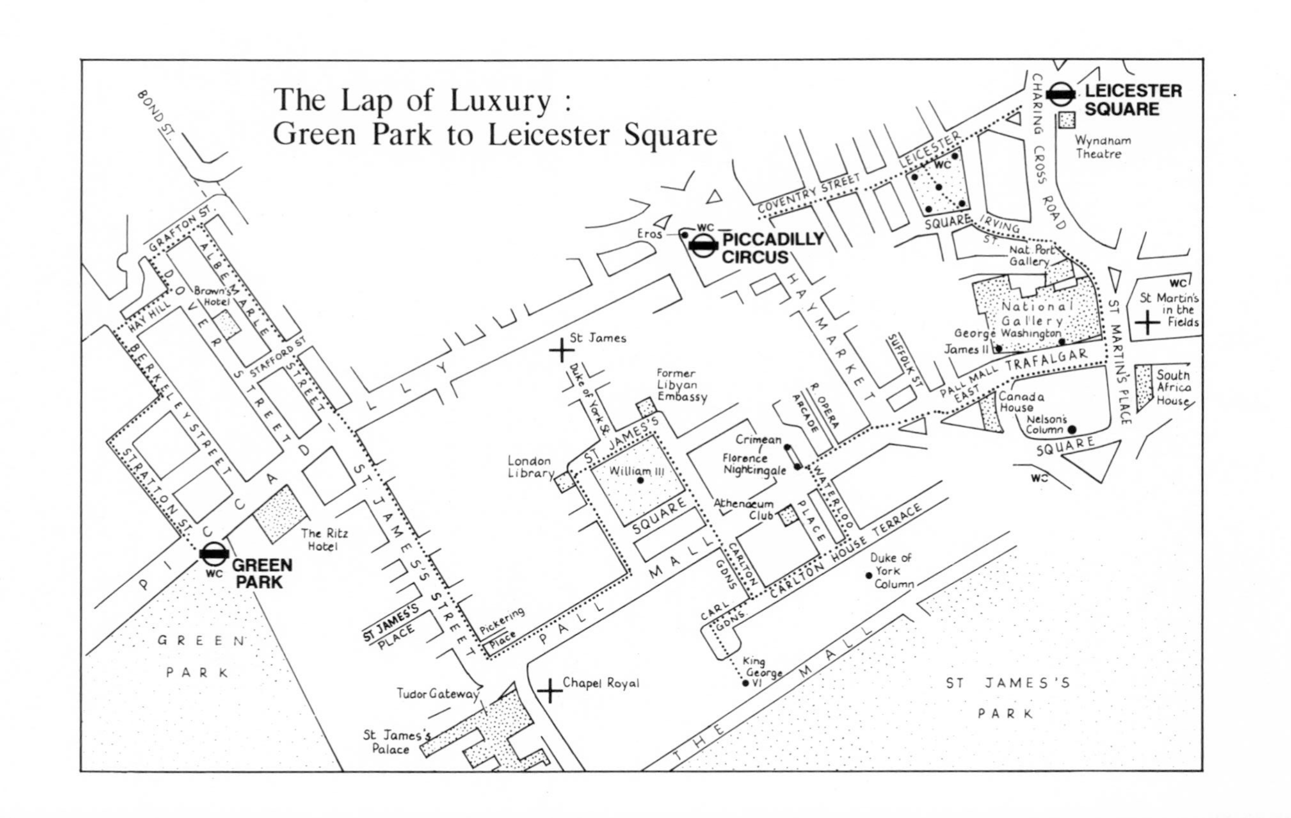
The Lap of Luxury :
Green Park to Leicester Square
LEICESTER SQUARE
Wyndham Theatre
CHARING CROSS ROAD
BOND ST.
GRAFTON ST.
ALBEMARLE
DOVER STREET
Brown's Hotel
HAY HILL
BERKELEY STREET
STRATTON ST.
STAFFORD ST
STREET
PICCADILLY
The Ritz Hotel
GREEN PARK
WC
ST JAMES'S STREET
ST JAMES'S PLACE
Pickering Place
Tudor Gateway
St James's Palace
Chapel Royal
St James
Duke of York St
London Library
ST JAMES'S SQUARE
William III
Former Libyan Embassy
PALL MALL
Eros
PICCADILLY CIRCUS
COVENTRY STREET
LEICESTER SQUARE
IRVING ST.
Nat. Port Gallery
National Gallery
George Washington
James II
HAYMARKET
SUFFOLK ST
R. OPERA ARCADE
Crimean
Florence Nightingale
Athenaeum Club
WATERLOO PLACE
CARLTON GDNS
CARL GDNS
King George VI
CARLTON HOUSE TERRACE
Duke of York Column
THE MALL
ST JAMES'S PARK
PALL MALL EAST
TRAFALGAR SQUARE
Canada House
Nelsons Column
ST MARTIN'S PLACE
St Martin's in the Fields
South Africa House

10

The Lap of Luxury: Green Park to Leicester Square

For most of this walk we shall be in St. James's - "Clubland" - where upmarket shops and auction houses specialize in the accoutrements and indulgences of the English elite lifestyle - fragrances, hats, shirts, shoes, wine, cigars, sporting guns, books, paintings, rare coins, and *objets d'art*; another ideal area for very upmarket window-shopping. This is a good walk for a showery day as it is quite short and there are lots of shops, galleries, and doorways to pop into if it rains.

Starting Point - North exit ("Royal Academy") Green Park station (Victoria, Piccadilly, and Jubilee lines)
You will emerge beside a car showroom, on the site of former Devonshire House (1737), which **Ben Franklin** visited and where in 1851 **Dickens** acted in a comedy before Queen Victoria. Its magnificent gates are *now to be seen on the opposite side of the road, down to your right*, set into the park railings but leading nowhere.

Before setting out, look across at Green Park, covering the site of a medieval leper hospital and devoid of flower beds. One story alleges that amorous Charles II habitually waylaid passing females with posies picked from the park, so his enraged queen, Catherine of Braganza, ordered the area to to be stripped of its flora. A more likely explanation is that lepers were buried in quicklime, which made the soil unsuitable for flowers. In 1748, Green Park was the setting for a pyrotechnic festival to mark the ending of the War of Austrian

Succession. Handel wrote *Music for the Royal Fireworks* for the occasion. *On the far side of the park you can see* the tower of Westminster Cathedral (RC) poking above the trees.

The Ritz Hotel *on the opposite side of Piccadilly* takes its name from its founder, **César Ritz**, who came to London as a humble Swiss waiter and ended up creating an establishment whose name became a by-word for stylish luxury, passing into the language as "ritzy." But his career ended in tragedy. In 1902, Ritz was commissioned to organize Edward VII's coronation banquet and scheduled his entire business year around the task. Unfortunately the king was stricken with appendicitis 48 hours before the big day, forcing the postponement of the coronation. Ritz had a nervous breakdown, from which he never fully recovered. When Hollywood stars **Douglas Fairbanks** and **Mary Pickford** stayed at the Ritz in 1920, they were besieged by besotted movie fans and had to flee to the country under police escort.

Turn right into Stratton St., to see fashionable Langan's Brasserie, co-founded by British film star Michael Caine. No. 1 Stratton St. was the home of **Angela Burdett-Coutts**, the richest woman in Victorian England. Advised by Charles Dickens, she sponsored many charities to help the poor, including assisted passages for those wanting to start a new life in North America. While still young Miss Burdett-Coutts proposed to the aged Duke of Wellington but did not finally get married until she was 67 – to an American less than half her age, with whom she was very happy. In 1905 the actor **Sir Henry Irving** lay "in state" in the drawing-room of No. 1, having died just up the street at No. 17.

Follow the right-hand bend of Stratton St., turn left into Berkeley St., right up Hay Hill and pause in Dover St. Down to your right, on the opposite side of the road stands sober, discreet Brown's Hotel, founded by Lord Byron's butler and much favored by Americans for generations.

Twenty-eight-year-old future President **Theodore Roosevelt** stayed here in 1886 before marrying at St. George's church in Hanover Square. His distant cousin, **Franklin D. Roosevelt**, honeymooned here in 1905. In 1907, **Mark Twain** stayed here before going up to Oxford to receive an honorary degree, alongside Kipling. Typically he took the opportunity to lampoon Brown's as the archetypal London hotel: "All the modern inconveniences are furnished, and some that have been obsolete for a century . . . The bedrooms are hospitals for incurable furniture . . . Some quite respectable Englishmen still frequent them through inherited habit and arrested development; many Americans also through ignorance and superstition." Aviator **Charles Lindbergh** was another regular patron here. Brown's Niagara Room recalls an historic meeting in 1890 when plans were agreed to develop the hydro-electric potential of the famous Falls.

Head north along Dover St. and pause opposite Nos. 3, 4, and 5, each of which retains period lamps with cone-shaped link-snuffers beneath them. In the eighteenth century, when streets were poorly lit and infested with muggers, prudent citizens venturing out by dark hired a boy to accompany them brandishing a link, a flaming length of tarred rope. On reaching their destination the linkboy snuffed out his torch and waited to accompany them back.

Turn right into Grafton St. and go to the end where there is a statue of **Churchill** and **Roosevelt**, sitting on a park bench, placed here to mark the 50th anniversary of the ending of World War Two. Up to the right, above Asprey's, the royal jewelers, a blue plaque marks where **Sir Henry Irving** lived in artistic chaos.

Retrace your steps and turn left into Albemarle Street. At No. 50 publisher **John Murray** introduced two of his most successful authors to each other - Lord Byron and Sir Walter Scott. Jane Austen was another of his stable.

Cross Piccadilly, head downhill along St. James's St. and

pause by the flight of steps and double lamps which mark the entrance to No. 37–8, White's, the oldest and grandest of all the St. James's clubs, which originated in 1693 (at No. 28) in the coffee and chocolate house run by an Italian, **Francesco Bianco** (who anglicized himself to Francis White). Past members include **Wellington** and the dandy **Beau Brummell**, who used to disport his finery in the bow window.

Continue and pause outside No. 28 at Boodle's. **Ian Fleming**, creator of James Bond, was once a member here. Both clubs were famed in the eighteenth century for marathon gambling sessions with absurdly high stakes.

Continue downhill until you come to Lobb's, supplier of boots and shoes to royalty and the very rich. Next door James Lock & Co. do the same with hats and were responsible for the invention of what the English call a "bowler" and Americans a "derby." The hat Wellington wore at the battle of Waterloo came from here.

Now look on the left for a narrow, shady passageway where a shiny plate informs you that this was once the site of a Legation representing the independent Republic of Texas from 1842 until it joined the United States in 1845. *At the end of the passage stands* charming Pickering Place, allegedly the site of the last duel fought in London.

Return to St. James's Street and observe the ancient, battered but impressive shop-front of Berry Bros. & Rudd. As the coffee-grinder shop sign suggests, this was not originally a wine merchant's but it had become one long before Byron and Brummell became regular customers. At No. 80 (now vanished) once stood the Thatched House Tavern where, in 1774, **Ben Franklin** and 28 other Americans met to protest the proposal to close the port of Boston as a punishment for the Boston Tea Party. Moderate in tone, their petition argued that this would punish the innocent along with the guilty. King, Lords, and Commons all received copies and ignored them - with momentous consequences.

Continue to the bottom of St. James's St. and pause to admire the fine brickwork of the Tudor gateway, the only surviving part of the original St. James's Palace. In 1785, **John Adams** presented his credentials here as independent America's first diplomatic representative in London and spoke warmly of his desire to restore the "old good nature and the old good humor between people, who, though separated by an ocean, and under different governments, have the same language, a similar religion and kindred blood." George III was visibly moved by Adams' "extremely proper" address, said he opposed the separation of the colonies only as a matter of royal duty, and, pledging friendship, took his cue from Adams to bid "the circumstances of language, religion and blood have their natural and full effect."

Turn left onto Pall Mall, named and originally laid out for paille-maille, the golf-cum-croquet game Charles II brought back with him from exile. *Walk on, past* Quebec House and *on the opposite side of the road*, Inigo Jones's Queen's Chapel (1623-7). At No. 79 a blue plaque marks the site of the former home of Charles II's favorite mistress, (Eleanor) **Nell Gwynne**. After she gave the king a son he failed to acknowledge paternity. Nell jogged his memory by threatening to drop the baby out of her top-floor window as the royal carriage passed by. Thoroughly alarmed, Charles hastily pleaded with her not to endanger the "Earl of Burford." On another occasion Nell's cheeky charm saved her. When an Oxford mob mistook her coach for that of one of the king's French, and therefore Catholic, mistresses and fell on it in a fury, Nell leaned out and bellowed, "Good people! I am the Protestant whore!" - and won a rousing round of cheers. *Next door stands the only original building in this street*, Schomberg House, where a blue plaque marks the studio of eminent portraitist **Thomas Gainsborough** (1727-88).

Continue eastwards along the north side of Pall Mall and turn left into St. James's Square. In the middle of the fine garden is a handsome equestrian statue of **William III**, the William of "William and Mary College," America's second oldest university, and Williamsburg, capital of colonial Virginia.

Walk along the left-hand side of the square to pass, in the northeast corner, the London Library, a private subscription library much used by British literati since its foundation by **Thomas Carlyle** in 1841. Carlyle himself regularly broke the most basic rules, refusing to return books when asked and scribbling scornful comments in the margins of books he disagreed with.

Continue along the north side of the square where there are two houses with blue plaques. No. 12 marks the former home of **Ada, Countess of Lovelace**, daughter of Lord Byron. A gifted mathematician, honored here as a pioneer of computing, she invented the "flow diagram" but wasted most of her time and fortune trying to devise a system for predicting winning horses. No. 10 is the home of the Royal Institute of International Affairs, established after World War One to bring the best brains from universities, diplomacy, the armed forces, business, and mass media to bear on international problems. Discussions are held under "Chatham House Rules" - participants may subsequently cite an opinion given there but may not specify by whom. Both No. 10 and the RIIA are known as "Chatham House" in honor of the first of three Prime Ministers who have lived there, **William Pitt the Elder**, Earl of Chatham.

Cross Duke of York Street and pause to look north at Sir Christopher Wren's fine church of St. James's, Piccadilly. *Continue along the north side of the Square to pause* outside No. 5., the "Libyan Arab People's Bureau" (i.e., Libyan Embassy) until 1982 when a crowd of peaceful demonstrators was fired on by one of the "diplomats." A young woman police constable, **Yvonne Fletcher**, on duty at the demonstration, was killed. Her memorial can be seen *at the foot of the railings on the opposite side of the road*. The Libyans claimed diplomatic immunity. No one was ever punished. Britain broke off diplomatic relations with Libya forthwith. A blue plaque on No. 4 marks the former home of **Nancy Astor**, the first woman to take her seat as an MP in the House of Commons. Nancy, wife of **William Waldorf Astor II**, was one of three Virginia-born Langhorn sisters who married into the English aristocracy; but she thought of herself as an aristocrat anyway, claiming descent from Pocahontas and proclaiming "I married beneath me. All women do." When her husband succeeded to a seat in the House of Lords on the death of W. W. Astor I, he had to renounce his seat in the Commons. Nancy fought and won it in 1919. In 1923, she became the first woman to introduce a bill into Parliament, banning bars from selling alcohol to under-18s. In a clash with **Winston Churchill**, she is alleged to have declared, "Winston, if I were married to you, I'd put poison in your coffee," provoking the instant retort, "Nancy, if I were married to you, I'd drink it."

Walk along the eastern side of the Square and pause outside neo-Georgian Norfolk House, where two plaques record its role as Eisenhower's planning headquarters for the invasions of North Africa (Operation Torch) and Normandy (Operation Overlord).

Leave the Square to cross Pall Mall and pass the Reform Club. Designed by **Charles Barry** (1837–41) on the lines of a classic Italian palazzo, its chaste lines became a model for a thousand banks and public buildings. The celebrated **Alexis Soyer** was chef here, the first leader of his profession to use gas-fired ovens for cooking. **Jules Verne**'s Phineas Fogg made his famous bet to go "round the world in eighty days" in the smoking-room of the Reform.

Continue up Carlton Gardens, turn right and then left until you are overlooking The Mall and St. James's Park by the statue of King George VI, the present Queen's father (reigned 1936–52), dressed in naval uniform (he had seen action at the Battle of Jutland in 1916). A slight, shy man with a marked speech hesitation, as second son of George V he never expected to be king. His playboy brother, groomed for the role, assumed the throne in 1936 as Edward VIII but abdicated within the year to marry American divorcee Mrs. Wallis Simpson and live in exile as the Duke of Windsor. Propelled reluctantly to the throne, George VI relied greatly on his wife, who "made him strong enough for her to lean on." *To the right, up the Mall, you can glimpse* Buckingham Palace. **Benjamin West** met George III here in 1768, when he was appointed his official History Painter. Queen Victoria invited a number of American entertainers here, including **Phineas T. Barnum's** "Col. Tom Thumb" and a minstrel choir. In 1918, **Woodrow Wilson** was the first President and first non-royal head of state to stay here. Saxophonist **Sidney Bechet** played for George V here in 1919 and stayed on for three years at a club in Tottenham Court Rd. During World War Two, George VI and his Queen repeatedly visited bombed-out areas during the Blitz. When the Palace itself was bombed the Queen is supposed to have said, "Now they have bombed my home I can look the East End in the face." When **Mrs. Roosevelt** stayed in the Palace during the war she found her bedroom freezing cold, as official fuel economies were scrupulously observed.

To the left of the statue as you are facing it a plaque marks the home of War Minister **Lord Kitchener** in World War One. Ferocious and devious, he was one of the few who saw that it would not be "over by Christmas." His heavily moustachioed face and accusing finger, calling for a million volunteers to serve "King and Country," adorned the most famous recruiting poster of the war and was adapted across the Atlantic to become "Uncle Sam Wants You for the U.S. Army."

In the shadow of 5 Carlton Gardens stands a statue of

A guard in summer undress uniform approaching Buckingham Palace c.1905. Sir Aston Webb refaced the facade in 1913 to give the Palace its present appearance.

General **Charles De Gaulle** (1890–1970), leader of the Free French forces during World War Two. Two plaques on No. 4 diagonally opposite explain the statue's location here. One gives the text of his historic broadcast of June 18, 1940 calling for continued resistance - which, apparently, very few people actually heard.

Retrace your footsteps into Carlton House Terrace and pause by the statue of **Lord Curzon.** A brilliant Orientalist scholar and diplomat, Curzon lived with acute pain and was forced to wear a steel corset for his twisted spine, which may account for his allegedly aloof, sneering manner. His devoted wife, American heiress **Mary Leiter**, accompanied him when he was Viceroy of India, where he lived more regally than a king, thanks to the Leiter millions, which also paid for their marital home at No. 1. Mary was warned by doctors that the Indian climate would kill her if she didn't go home. She wouldn't and it did. (James Bond fans will remember that his CIA contact is Felix Leiter. Ian Fleming, as snobbish as Bond, doubtless assumed that the American secret services, like the British, only recruited from the elite.) Curzon became Foreign Secretary but never achieved the Premiership he thought his due.

Continue along Carlton House Terrace. Around 1900, this was *the* address to have and was positively clogged with American heiresses, who lived at Nos. 3, 5, 7, 18, 20, and 22. U.S. Ambassador **Hay** rented No. 5 during his tour of duty in 1897–8. Ambassador **Choate** took the Curzons' house while they were in India. In 1922 press baron **Lord Northcliffe** died at No. 2, barking mad, having lived his last days in a little hut on the roof. The fifth **Earl of Lonsdale** (1857–1944) occupied Nos. 14 *and* 15. The "sporting Earl" once knocked out the American world heavyweight champion John L. Sullivan. A coal mining fortune enabled him to spend £3,000 a year on cigars alone. Edward VII dismissed him as "almost an Emperor but not *quite* a gentleman." Canadian-born **Sir Gilbert Parker** (1862–1932), novelist and historian of Quebec, lived at No. 20 with his American wife. His baronetcy was given for services to "war propaganda in the United States."

Stop in Waterloo Place and note the statue of explorer **Sir John Franklin**, who died, with his entire expedition, seeking to find a Northwest Passage from the Atlantic to the Pacific through Canada's Arctic waters. The plinth shows the ill-fated explorers burying some of their comrades. Thirty-two expeditions were sent out to discover their fate.

Towering above this area is the Duke of York's column. An incompetent general, better known for scandalous love affairs, he nonetheless inspired far-distant Toronto to change its name to York in his honor - and after his death change back.

Cross to the opposite side of Waterloo Place where, in full polar kit, you can see the memorial to **Captain Robert Falcon Scott**, sculpted by his widow. "Scott of the Antarctic" vowed to be first at the South Pole but, when he reached it, found the Norwegian flag already flying there. Beaten by Raold Amundsen, Scott and his comrades man-hauled their dwindling supplies 800 miles back, only to die in a blizzard less than ten miles from a food dump. A stirring extract from Scott's diary is reproduced on the plinth of the statue.

Look back across Waterloo Place to the cream-painted Athenaeum Club, whose entrance is surmounted by golden Pallas Athene, guardian deity of ancient Athens and goddess of Wisdom, Industry, and War. Note around the top of the building a reproduction of the festival procession which provides the main motif of the "Elgin Marbles," now in the British Museum. The members actually wanted an ice house rather than this adornment but the club's forceful founder prevailed:

> I'm John Wilson Croker
> I do as I please
> They ask for an ice house
> I'll give them a frieze.

The Athenaeum has long been considered the most intellectual of London clubs. **Emerson** felt honored to be granted temporary membership, a privilege given to only ten foreigners at any one time. **Teddy Roosevelt** was also an honorary member. **Henry James** liked to use the fine library and take part in the afternoon ritual when "the divinest salvers of tea and buttered toast" were served up by "amiable flunkies in knee-breeches." Other literary members have included Thackeray, Kipling, Barrie, Conan Doyle, and Galsworthy.

Just across Pall Mall, in Waterloo Place, you can see the imposing memorial to the dead of the Crimean War, fought against Russia in 1854–6. *To the left in front of it stands* a statue of **Florence Nightingale**, "the lady with the lamp" (shown carrying the wrong sort of lamp), founder of modern nursing. *To the left note* British Columbia House at the corner of Charles II St. In 1849, impoverished American painter **George Catlin** rented a studio here to display his unique collection of paintings of Native American life. Sir Thomas Phillipps gave him temporary salvation by commissioning 55 copies at £2 a time. Catlin died destitute in 1872 but his "Indian Gallery" did eventually end up in the Smithsonian.

Cross Pall Mall, turn right and glance down the lamp-lit Royal Opera Arcade, one of London's earliest shopping malls (1817). New Zealand House stands on the former site of the Carlton Hotel. **César Ritz** became manager here after leaving the Savoy with renowned chef Escoffier, after a row about kickbacks from kitchen suppliers. A blue plaque just round the corner on the Haymarket frontage records that **Ho Chi Minh**, founder of modern Vietnam, once worked here in the kitchens.

Cross the road at the bottom of Haymarket, pass into Pall Mall East and note the statue of **George III**, amiably waving his hat and ignoring the Texas Embassy café behind him. *Cross Suffolk St.* and spare a thought for free trade fanatic **Richard Cobden** MP, who died at No. 23 in 1865, having come up to London, in defiance of his doctor, specifically to denounce a proposal to spend money on strengthening the fortifications of Quebec and Montreal. A fervent admirer of free enterprise America, Cobden took a dim view of Canada as impoverished and backward, clinging timidly to the "mother country." Cobden thought defending Canada from the United States was both impossible and unnecessary but asthma felled him before he could denounce the Anglo-Canadian link as a "sham" which would "snap asunder if it should ever be put to the strain of stern reality." Well, he *was* wrong about *that*, wasn't he?

Continue past the Sainsbury Wing of the National Gallery (paid for by the Sainsbury's food supermarket family and designed by American architect **Robert Venturi**) and pause in front of the statue of **James II** (reigned 1685–8), attributed to Wren's master-carver **Grinling Gibbons**. James, a convert to Catholicism, was

The last King of America – George III turns his back on the Texas Embassy Café.

deposed for foisting his faith on his Protestant subjects. In younger days, as Duke of York, he was a brave and capable admiral and when New Amsterdam was taken from the Dutch in 1664, it was renamed New York in his honor.

Looking out over Trafalgar Square you can see Nelson's Column and *to the right*, Canada House. Originally built in 1825 as headquarters of the Royal College of Physicians by **Sir Robert Smirke**, Scottish architect of the British Museum, it was taken over by the Canadian High Commission a century later. *Opposite*, South Africa House occupies the former site of hundred-bedroom Morley's Hotel, much favored by generations of American visitors from 1831 until 1921, when it was demolished. Vermont-born book-dealer **Henry Stevens** did all his business from Morley's. In the course of 40 years he secured over 100,000 items of Americana for the British Museum. His greatest single coup was to find 3,000 of Ben Franklin's manuscripts in a room over a St. James's tailor-shop.

Pass in front of the National Gallery and pause in front of the statue of **George Washington.** Donated in 1921 by the Commonwealth of Virginia, this is a replica of the life-size original by French sculptor Houdon, which stands in the capitol at Richmond. Washington is shown holding an empty scabbard, having put aside his sword. Behind him is a plough, symbolically referring to his resumption of private life at Mount Vernon after victory in the Revolutionary War, like the Roman hero Cincinnatus, who left his plough to defend his country and then modestly returned to it, shunning honors, after he had done his duty. Survivors of the Revolutionary War founded the world's oldest veterans' organization and called it the Order of Cincinnatus - hence Cincinnatti, Ohio. Notice that the column on which the statue leans is in the form of an ancient Roman *fasces*, symbol of civic authority, and has 13 visible facets, one for each of the rebel colonies. Between them are arrows, emblematic of America's native peoples.

Turn the corner and note opposite the church of St. Martin-in-the-Fields. Combining the deep portico of a Greek temple with a Christian spire, it was thought bizarre when it was designed by the Scottish Catholic **James Gibbs** in 1722–4 but it has since provided the inspiration for many New England churches. American painter **Benjamin West** was married here in 1765. A century later P. T. Barnum's prize giantess, 7′ 6″ **Anna Swan** from Nova Scotia, married Kentuckian **Van Bern Bates**, who was just three-and-a-half inches shorter than her. Queen Victoria presented the bride with a gold watch. Notable burials include those of Nell Gwynne,

John Henry Brodribb, or Sir Henry Irving, as he preferred to be known. Irving was the first actor to be honored with a knighthood.

Hogarth, Reynolds, and Chippendale. The Church is now noted for its music.

Continue past the National Portrait Gallery to pause by the statue of **Sir Henry Irving**, the first actor to be knighted and a theatrical hero on both sides of the Atlantic, particularly noted for his scholarly revivals of Shakespeare and his long-standing liaison with stage partner Ellen Terry.

Pass through Irving St. into Leicester Square. At its four corners stand busts of local residents. Scientist **Sir Isaac Newton** once lived where Westminster Library stands to the south. **Hogarth's** house was at the corner of Irving Street, now a Chinese restaurant. **Sir Joshua Reynolds'** fine house and studio once stood opposite.

Leicester Square c.1904. The layout of the gardens has since been changed to diagonal paths. Notice the telegraph pole looming up from the buildings on the right.

The fourth local resident, **John Hunter** (1728–93), was the founder of comparative anatomy. *In the middle of the square stands* a copy of Scheemakers' Westminster Abbey memorial to **Shakespeare** – opposite sprightly London-born **Charlie Chaplin.** *Around the railings of the central area* are bronze handprints in the sidewalk. One set (including Charlton Heston and Omar Sharif) commemorate British Film Year (1985), the other (Sylvester Stallone, Bruce Willis, Arnold Schwarzenegger) the opening of Planet Hollywood (1993).

Exit Leicester Square east via Cranbourn St. to reach Leicester Square station (Northern line). On the corner is the former Hippodrome music hall (look up to see an emblematic chariot still in place). In 1913, **Irving Berlin**, crossing the Atlantic, whiled away the time writing *Alexander's Ragtime Band*, which was first performed at the Hippodrome and took London by storm. During

Piccadilly Circus c.1910. A Japanese flag hangs from a building at the corner of Shaftesbury Ave (left). A newly-built Japanese department store, Sogo (1992) now occupies the site between the Criterion and the Haymarket on the right.

World War Two the Hippodrome housed the Rainbow Club, a rendezvous for U.S. and other Allied servicemen.

Alternatively, exit west via Coventry Street to pass Planet Hollywood and reach Piccadilly Circus station (Piccadilly and Bakerloo lines). Walk ends.

En Route: Richard Recommends

Food and Drink

Tea at the Ritz is an experience but Brown's is less flashy, more cozy, more English. Gaylord in Albemarle St. offers top-rate Indian food; in the same street is self-service Granary, especially attractive to vegetarians. There are good cafeterias in St. James's church, Piccadilly and in the crypt of St. Martin-in-the-Fields. Pedestrianized Irving Street at the end of the walk has a variety of cheap eateries (pizza, kebabs, Chinese, Indian, Tibetan), as does the whole Leicester Sq. area.

Public Toilets

Green Park station (south side). Trafalgar Square (underpass, south side). Leicester Sq. (north side).

Delays and Diversions

Canadian War Memorial (1994), Green Park. Leave Green Park station (south exit), pass the bandstand and you should see it, to the right, before you reach Canada Gate. The memorial is aligned with Halifax, Nova Scotia, from which town so many Canadian troops departed in both world wars.

At 21 Albemarle St., in **Michael Faraday's** actual laboratory, the Royal Institution preserves the manuscripts, personal possessions, and experimental apparatus of the scientist whose studies transformed electricity from a curiosity of nature into a practicable form of energy. Open 1–4 Mon.–Fri. (£.)

Off the west side of St. James's St., down St. James's Place, stands magnificent Spencer House, a miniature Versailles (£). En route note the plaques recording the temporary London home (No. 4) of Polish piano maestro **Chopin** (1810–49) (the damp London atmosphere finished off his never-too-sturdy lungs) and of **Sir Francis Chichester** (1901–72) (see p. 16). American humorist **James Thurber** stayed three times at the Stafford Hotel, just round the corner, at 16 St. James's Place, and was much lionized by the London press. **James Fenimore Cooper** took No. 33 for a couple of months in 1828 to finish *Notions of the Americans*.

The National Gallery (Trafalgar Sq.) houses some 2,000 world-class pictures, covering European painting from 1300 to the 20th century. Despite its name, the National Portrait Gallery (rear of National Gallery) is not strictly limited to Britons and contains much of specifically Canadian interest. Apart from portraits of numerous venerable governors and viceroys, there is a bust of **Sir John A. Macdonald**, the father of Confederation, a splendid painting of newspaper tycoon **Beaverbrook** by **Walter Sickert**, two paintings and a bust of Arctic explorer **Franklin**, and no less than four pictures and a bust of **Wolfe**, captor of Quebec.

Shopping and Souvenirs

Bond St., Jermyn St., and the arcades leading off them are lined with luxury shops. There are also well-stocked shops in the National Gallery, National Portrait Gallery, and the crypt of St. Martin-in-the-Fields. The Charing Cross Road branch of Westminster public library (next to the Garrick Theatre) has a stall specialising in Sherlock Holmes books, pamphlets, and memorabilia.

A Guide's Guide to Guides

There are specialized guidebooks on London's shops, theaters, pubs, and restaurants which are up-dated annually. A full reading list on London's history can be found in my *A Traveller's History of London* (Windrush Press/Interlink 1992).

Specifically American aspects are covered in:

Hazelton, F. *London's American Past* (Papermac, 1991), written as a series of guided walks

MacColl, G. and Wallace, C. McD. *To Marry an English Lord* (Sidgwick and Jackson, 1989)

Morton, B. N. *Americans in London* (Macdonald/Queen Anne Press, 1986), a biographical dictionary organized on a street-by-street basis.

Canadian links are covered in:

Simpson, J. and Martin, G. *The Canadian Guide to Britain: Volume One, England* (Macmillan of Canada, 1985).

For the general background to transatlantic relations see:

Dimbleby, D. and Reynolds, D. *An Ocean Apart* (BBC/Hodder and Stoughton, 1988)

Frost, D. and Shea, M. *The Rich Tide: Men, Women, Ideas and their Transatlantic Impact* (Collins, 1986)

Recent publications on London include:

Histories

Porter, R. *London: A Social History* (Hamish Hamilton, 1994)
Billings, M. *London: A Companion to Its History and Archaeology* (Kyle Cathie, 1994)
Richardson, J. *London and Its People* (Barrie and Jenkins, 1995)

Anthologies

Bailey, P. *The Oxford Book of London* (Oxford University Press, 1995)
Saint, A. and Darley, G. *The Chronicles of London* (Weidenfeld & Nicolson, 1994)
Wilson, A. N. *The Faber Book of London* (Faber & Faber, 1993)

Ethnic Aspects

Mann, K. *London: The German Connection* (KT Publishing, 1993)
McAuley, I. *Guide to Ethnic London* (Immel Publishing, 1993)
Merriman, N. (ed) *The Peopling of London* (Museum of London, 1993)

Architecture

Allinson, K and Thornton, V. *A Guide to London's Contemporary Architecture* (Butterworth, 1993)
Harwood, E. and Saint, A. *Exploring England's Heritage: London* (English Heritage/HMSO, 1991)

Themes

Berkeley, R. *A Spy's London* (Leo Cooper, 1994)

Hallgarten, E. and Collister, L. *The Gourmet's Guide to London* (Vermilion, 1992)
Linford, J. *Food Lovers' London* (Metro Publications, 1995)
Rosen, D. and S. *London Science* (Prion, 1994)
Schreuders, P., Lewisohn, M., and Smith, A. *The Beatles' London* (Hamlyn, 1994)
Weightman, G. *Bright Lights, Big City: London Entertained 1830–1950* (Collins & Brown, 1992)

Specific Areas

Grynberg, W. *The Square Mile: The City of London in Historic Postcards* (Windrush Press, 1995)
Tames, R. *Bloomsbury Past* (Historical Publications, 1993)
Tames, R. *Soho Past* (Historical Publications, 1994)
Tames, R. *The City of London Past* (Historical Publications, 1995)
Weightman, G. *London River: The Thames Story* (Collins and Brown, 1990)

Walking Tours

Booth, F. *The Independent Walker's Guide to Great Britain* (Interlink/Windrush, 1996)
Duncan, A. *Walking London* (New Holland, 1991)
Duncan, A. *Secret London* (New Holland, 1995)
Mason, M. and Sanders, M. *The City Companion* (Robert Hale, 1994)
Pepper, C. *Walks in Oscar Wilde's London* (Gibbs Smith, 1992)
Wittich, J. *Explorer's London* (Morning Mist Publications, 1995)

Index

Other titles of interest

The Independent Walker series

The Independent Walker's Guide to Great Britain
The Independent Walker's Guide to France

The Traveller's History series

A Traveller's History of China
A Traveller's History of England
A Traveller's History of France
A Traveller's History of Greece
A Traveller's History of India
A Traveller's History of Ireland
A Traveller's History of Italy
A Traveller's History of Japan
A Traveller's History of London
A Traveller's History of North Africa
A Traveller's History of Paris
A Traveller's History of Russia
A Traveller's History of Scotland
A Traveller's History of Spain
A Traveller's History of Turkey

For a complete catalog of travel titles please write to:

In the U.S. :
Interlink Publishing Group, Inc.
46 Crosby Street
Northampton, MA 01060-1804
U.S.A.
Tel: (413) 582 7054
Fax: (413) 582 7057
e-mail: interpg@aol.com

In the U.K. :
The Windrush Press
Little Window
High Street, Moreton-in-Marsh
Gloucestershire, GL56 OLL
England
Tel: 01608 652012
Fax: 01608 652125